Beautifully
UNDONE

Beautifully UNDONE

THE BEAUMONT BROTHERS

SUSAN GRISCOM

Beautifully Undone is a work of fiction. All of the characters, organizations, and events portrayed in this novel are either products of the author's imagination or are used fictitiously.

Copyright © 2016 by Susan Griscom

www.susangriscom.com

Edited by Michelle Leah Olson
Cover designed by Susan Griscom

ISBN-13: 978-1523321353

Other works by Susan Griscom

Sand and Sunset Series
Broken Wide Open

The Beaumont Brothers
Beautifully Wounded, Book 1
Beautifully Used, Book 2
Beautifully Undone, Book 3

Paranormal Romance
Immortal Hearts of San Francisco
Tempted by a Vampire
Captivated by a Vampire
Rocked by a Vampire
Possessed by a Vampire

The Whisper Cape Trilogy
Paranormal Romance
Whisper Cape, Book 1
Reflections, Book 2
A Secret Fate, Book 3

Single Titles

A Gypsy's Kiss (Paranormal Romance)

Allusive Aftershock (A Young Adult Romance/Dystopian)

Beautifully Undone

He was broken.

Full of hate and sorrow.

Asher Beaumont never asked for much in life. All he wanted was to play his guitar, write music, and be recognized and loved by his father. Unfortunately, that last desire was never realized. The bastard died when Asher was just a kid. Then thirteen years later, his mother dies of a brain tumor, shattering him even more and leaving him hating everyone around him, except for his two best friends, Melody Stevens and her brother, Teddy.

Melody Stevens has crushed on her best friend, Asher Beaumont her entire life. But it's always been a secret passion. Never something she'd act upon. But when she tells Asher she's prepared—and determined—to lose her virginity to a guy he considers to be nothing more than a cad who sleeps with anything that wears a skirt, her best friend offers her a proposition she can't really refuse.

When Asher stumbles across a letter left by his mother before her death, begging him to seek out his half-brothers, he and Melody begin a journey of discovery. Their travels lead them to the two brothers he has spent his life despising because they had the life he always wanted. While on their trip, they discover a miracle they never, ever considered.

A Stand-alone, third book in The Beaumont Brothers series with a HEAfor Adults 18+

Dear Readers,

This book started taking flight soon after Brodie's story, when I realized I didn't want the Beaumont brothers to end quite yet, my mind began to imagine all sorts of possibilities. When I started writing Asher's story, I knew exactly what I wanted and where it would end up, even all the in between stuff. Both Asher's and Melody's characters flowed into my imagination as if I'd lived their lives myself, though I didn't.

You can find the first and second books on Amazon and all three are free in the Kindle Unlimited program.

Beautifully Wounded, Book 1, Jackson and Lena
Beautifully Used, Book 2, Brodie and Gabrielle
Beautifully Undone, Book 3, Asher and Melody

All three of these stories deal with real life situations and social issues. I've tried my best to keep it as real as possible, of course, it is fiction, and I do like to have a happily ever after at the end of all my stories. Just a warning, the sex scenes get steamier with each book. Sorry, I just couldn't help it.

It takes a strong individual to bounce back from some of the horrors of real life, and I believe I've portrayed that in these stories. Never give up hope, because I truly believe you are what you make of yourself and we are all in control of our own situations. Be brave, be strong, and don't ever let someone tell you that you can't do something or that you're not good enough to do something that you have a passion for.

I hope you love Asher and Melody as much as I do.

Beautifully UNDONE

THE BEAUMONT BROTHERS

Chapter One

Asher

I didn't believe in ghosts. Well, not completely. I believed in spirits. If you told me that every being who ever died came back and roamed the earth for eternity...I'd have to disagree. No way could I ever believe that the monster who'd sired me was lurking around, propagating meritless inspiration to all mankind. That'd almost be as bad as saying Hitler roamed the earth, whispering hideous political objectives, advocating anti-Semitism into the ears of unsuspecting politicians. At least, I'd like to believe all that. I did hope that the song emanating from my lips transcended the here and now, radiating a comforting repose into space, and somehow captured the loving ears of my mother.

As I strummed the guitar, softly singing the words, I looked up. A crowd began to form, spanning the entire area from where I sat perched upon a sidewalk bench, all the way to the edge of the wall separating them from the unforgiving cold bay as they huddled around me, listening. Wind whipped locks of my hair into my face and licked at my fingertips as I dexterously progressed through the chords of the song. The tune, a ballad, one I'd written myself, poured from my lips with a smooth, heartfelt rhythm. Words that told a story, my story, but no one knew that. No one would ever guess that.

A woman holding the hand of a toddler stepped forward and dropped a buck into the hat that sat a few feet in front of me. I smiled at her as I sang.

I didn't usually perform on the streets of San Francisco. I had a regular nightly gig at a nightclub on the wharf, but today, I'd felt the need to sit and watch people. Then I'd needed to just play my guitar, sing a soft tune—only to console myself. I hadn't intended to draw a crowd, nor take in any money. That's not why my hat was there. It had blown off my head a few minutes into the song and had rather conveniently landed rim-side-up directly in front of my feet. By my calculations, I would guess there were about thirty dollars in there now. I was on my second song already, but I hadn't had the heart to pick up my hat and leave after the first one ended. I would have liked to just walk away and continue with my grief in private. Except people lingered, their attention directed at me, my words, my music. Their ears tuned to my voice, my guitar. Expectant. I wasn't one to disappoint. I'd give them their show for another fifteen minutes. Then I'd be on my way, walk a few blocks west toward the beach, maybe stare at the sea for a while.

My plan was to sit and watch the seals, the people, the surroundings, everything happening around me before taking the Muni toward the Golden Gate Bridge. There I would wait, until life quieted down. Until people left with their friends and families in tow to dinner. Then, in the calm, the quiet hour of dusk, I would sprinkle her ashes. Let them trickle out slowly as I walked along the edge of the bridge. That's what she would have wanted. She didn't need people to mourn her; I didn't need people to console me. My mother hadn't been a needy person.

The hand on my shoulder startled me, but I kept on playing as I glanced up and saw Mel's worried face. Her smile—timid, yet sweet. She sat down next to me, and with her own guitar resting across her lap, proceeded to strum the chords along with me without skipping a beat. She was miraculous that way, gifted with a talent beyond imagination. Her parents had known what they were doing when they'd given her that name.

Melody was my best friend. We'd been friends ever since she and I were babies—we were only a week apart in age, though I was older. Ted, my other best friend and Mel's brother, was a year older than us, and the three of us had grown up together. Our mothers were best friends. Mel, Ted, and their mother had moved into the house next door to mine in San Mateo when Mel and I were four years old. Her mom still lived there. As did mine, up until last week anyway.

Mel gave me a dubious glance and raised her eyebrows in question when a woman dropped a couple of bills into the hat that still sat on the ground in front of me. I only shrugged and continued to play. After the song had ended, the crowd applauded, and several more people stepped forward to give their donations to the hat. Mel let out a small giggle, and I nodded at them, thanking each one.

When I didn't start up a new song, the crowd slowly began to disperse. I turned to Mel. "What are you doing here?"

"You need me," Mel retorted.

"No, I don't. You shouldn't have followed me."

"I can't let you do this on your own, Ash. You would never let me if it was the other way around and you know it."

She was right about that, but I didn't want her with me this time. I had to do it on my own. I had to say goodbye on my own. "Just go home. I'll come over after. You can help me go through all her stuff tomorrow if you want, but this, *this* I need to do by myself."

"I loved her too, you know," she pouted.

"I know you did. But I can't..." I couldn't explain to her how hard this was going to be for me. That I needed to be alone in case I lost it. That would only make her want to go with me even more.

She put her hand on my arm. "Ash, you need me."

"Don't." I glanced up at her, my eyes heavy with the threat of moisture. I couldn't let her see my tears. They needed to be private. I glanced back down at my hands. I stood and started packing up my guitar, and she packed up hers, as well. Just because she and I were very close, and I could tell her just about anything, didn't mean I could share this with her. I was all my mom had, and she was all I had. Sure, I had Melody, for now, but what would happen when she finally met her prince? I didn't think we'd be able to continue like we were. Be as close when that happened—if she were my girlfriend, in a romantic way, I'd never stand for another man being her best friend—and then where would that leave me? Alone. So, I needed to do this solo.

"Okay. I get it. You think I don't, but I do. When you're done, come find me, I'll buy you an Irish Coffee to take the chill off." She turned and hurried away. I swallowed the lump that had built up in my throat and rubbed the wetness from my eyes before it had a chance to escape and took off toward the bridge.

The sun was sinking in the sky, and it would only be another few minutes before it dropped down completely behind the horizon. My mother had loved this time of day. She said it always made her feel like God was painting the heavens just for us to admire. I had to agree as I studied the purple and blood-red-orange of the sky. There were just enough clouds to make it a truly spectacular sunset. One she would have loved.

The bridge was fairly empty now as the sun disappeared completely, leaving nothing but the beautiful pastel hues canvassing the sky. It would only be a matter of minutes before darkness took over and the walkway on the bridge would close to pedestrians so I needed to be quick. I walked along the pathway until I reached the middle of the bridge and stopped, glancing around for any late, lingering sightseers as I reached into my backpack to pull out the urn that held my mom's ashes. I stood, resting the gold-colored jar on the top of the railing and looked out over the bay as it flowed into the ocean on the west side of the bridge. Cars whizzed by in each direction in the middle of the structure. It was rush hour, and even though the number of pedestrians had diminished, the traffic leaving and coming into the city was horrendous.

"I know this is what you wanted, Mom, and I promised to do it." I took in a deep breath of air and exhaled with a heavy sigh. I opened the urn and glanced inside at the ashes that used to be my mother. I held the jar out over the water, ready to release the ashes, but my hands wouldn't turn it over to let them spill out. I pulled the urn back and sank down on the cement walkway, leaning my back against one of the metal pillars that was close by. I studied the urn in my hands. Why was I having so much trouble letting go? It wasn't like she was in the jar. I looked inside. Nothing but ashes.

I'd said my goodbyes to her in the hospital before she died, held her hand and watched her slip away. Her last breath coming out in a small sputter. It was the hardest thing I'd ever had to do. Later that same day, I'd had to go to the mortuary to identify her body since I was her only living relative. They'd said it was a formality, even though I'd been present when she died, the mortuary still needed a relative to identify her before they could cremate her remains.

It was getting darker, and before long, the gates on the bridge would lock. I'd be forced to try and climb them if I didn't hurry. Not something I wanted to do since I'd probably have my ass hauled off to jail. I bent my head down and stared into the urn, then closed my eyes and tried to picture my mom's face. Her blue eyes so full of hope, even when there wasn't any. She was an optimist, and according to her, the glass was always three-quarters full of champagne.

When the tumor in her brain became too large, it had started to give her hallucinations. I'd sometimes find her lying in the bed talking to my father, who, of course, was never there. He hadn't been around since I was four years old. He wasn't always a total jerk, though. He'd sent my mom a few hundred dollars every month, but his main focus had always been on his "real" family. The one he'd had prior to meeting my mom and knocking her up with me. He'd never made any big promises to her about leaving that family and living with us, so maybe that made him somewhat honorable. Although, I didn't know under whose definition that would fall. Certainly not mine.

I remember being a little kid, crying one day as he was leaving to go home to his other family. I'd begged him to take me with him. He'd told me I had two big brothers, and I'd wanted to meet them. Emphasis on the past tense in that last thought, since the desire to meet them and be part of that fucked up family had ended a long time ago. That was the last time I'd seen my father. When I was about eight, we'd heard through distant friends that he'd been in a horrific auto accident and passed away in the ambulance on the way to the hospital. That news came shortly after the monthly checks had stopped coming.

With the urn positioned upright between my legs and my elbows resting on my thighs, I lowered my head into my hands. *God, why is this so much harder than I thought it would be?*

I should have been surprised when the slight weight of an arm draped over my shoulders, but I wasn't. Melody knew me better than I knew myself.

"I told you, you needed me."

I swiped the wetness from my cheeks and let her pull my head against her shoulder, allowing her to become a temporary reprieve from the grief that I hadn't released yet. Until that moment, I hadn't realized that I'd been lacking in the solace that she so eagerly wanted to give me. I squeezed my eyes shut and just took comfort in her sweetness. A sweetness bordering on intimacy that had always only been at the surface of our relationship but never penetrable. Always forbidden in our minds.

When I finally found my voice and was able to speak without choking on my words, I lifted my head. "You're right. Thanks."

"When are you going to learn to listen to me?" she asked.

I shook my head. "Never."

"Right, because I'm just a girl and girls don't know anything."

I laughed. That was something I'd said to her when we were about eleven years old, and she'd never let me forget it. It had been right around the time we'd vowed to marry each other when we grew up. In sixth grade, we'd actually kissed. It was her twelfth birthday, and spin the bottle was the game of choice. Parental supervision had been scarce, and everyone was taking advantage of it. It was my turn and I spun the bottle. I'd closed my eyes, not wanting it to point to anyone except Melody, and was pleasantly surprised when it stopped and aimed directly at her. I remembered her sheepish smile as I scooted close to her. When my lips had touched hers, everyone started counting. The longer the count, the more noise everyone made. I believe we made it to twenty-five before I opened my eyes and slowly drew back.

Except, after that day, neither one of us had ever dared to bring up that kiss again. In fact, the topic remained so far off the table that we'd never even dated as teenagers or become romantically involved in any sense of the term. Now that we were twenty-one, Mel and I were still best friends.

Chapter Two

Melody

"Come on," I tugged Ash's arm to get him to stand up. "It's getting dark and they're going to close the gate soon."

He clutched the urn in his arm and stood. We looked out over the railing. It was a long way down there. I almost started to step back. My slight fear of heights had a tingle creeping up my spine, but I knew he needed me to stay close.

I leaned over and glanced inside the urn at the ashes.

"She's really gone." His soft words were almost lost on the ocean breeze.

I nodded. "She'd love what you are doing. You know that."

"I do."

"We should say something."

"Yes." He looked at me and straightened his shoulders as if he were going to make a big long speech. I smiled.

"Nora Becket, my mom, was the best mother anyone could ever have. She was always there for me, and she loved life and fought so hard up until the very end. I'll miss you, Mom, so very much." His last sentence came out on a raspy sob. "Rest in peace," he finished.

"Goodbye, Nora. I'll always love you. Thank you for being the best second mom anyone could ever have," I said. "And thanks for never telling my mom about us ditching school in tenth grade." Ash chuckled and swiped at his eyes. It had been during a one-day teacher strike, and substitutes had had to take over all of our classes. Ash had said screw it, they'd never miss us, so he and I had taken off to the beach right after first period. Everything would have been fine, even with the sunburned faces we'd gotten, except for the sand that Ash had forgotten to rinse out of his short's pockets. Sunburns were easy to explain since our lunches were always taken outside. We'd told our moms that we'd both fallen asleep during our lunch hours. A May sunny day in San Francisco was rare, so they'd bought it, knowing how much we all loved soaking up the sun on those days. Until Nora did laundry and found the sand in Asher's pocket. She'd questioned him about it, and he'd fessed up. She'd lectured me too, giving us both the "why we shouldn't ditch school again, and what the consequences would be if we did" talk, but she never ratted me out to my mom. I did eventually tell my mom about it, but not until after graduation.

I placed my hands around the urn below his, and together, we tilted the porcelain jar and watched the ashes spill out as they floated their way down to the water. The wind blew several back up and they hit us in the face. We both spit the ashes away from our lips and wiped our mouths with the backs of our hands.

Ash smiled. "She's still a fighter."

"That's for sure."

"Thanks for following me, Mel. It was easier having you here."

"You're welcome." It didn't surprise me that he needed me, but it did surprise me that he'd admitted it.

He placed the empty urn in his backpack and slung the guitar case over his other shoulder. I took my case and did the same, then I took his hand as we walked toward the end of the bridge.

"I'll let you buy me that Irish Coffee you promised me now. I think my fingers are about to fall off they're so cold," I said.

"If I remember correctly, and I think I do, it was you who offered to buy *me* the coffee."

I shrugged. "Yeah, but you have more money than I do."

The coffee house was jam-packed with wall-to-wall people. It was Friday night, and the city was already booming with weekend tourists. We made our way to the counter after standing in line for about ten minutes, and Ash ordered two Irish Coffees, one heavy on the whipped cream; that was his. The more whipped cream, the better as far as he was concerned.

"Mmmm…" I hummed as the smooth, sweet cream mixed with the coffee and whiskey goodness warmed my throat. Ash laughed, and I frowned when I looked up at him as his finger swiped across the tip of my nose. He held up his whipped-cream-covered fingertip before sticking it in his mouth, sucking it dry. My stomach jittered then knotted.

Wow. He was so sexy. I'd always thought so, but now, in this light, his green eyes twinkled and his tanned face made him look just like one of the cover model guys I drooled over in my escape world of reading romance novels. My heart thumped and I had to look away, trying to focus on something less…Asher.

I needed to concentrate on something real. Not that Ash wasn't real. But, I mean, a real, possible relationship. The only problem was, most guys I knew were friends with Ash and always treated me as if I were one of the guys, just like Ash did.

I once overheard Asher tell Brent that he'd pummel the life out of any guy who ever tried to get into my pants. Not that getting into my pants was ever going to happen with any of those runts, but he did manage to scare the crap out of all of them whenever the subject of me came up. It used to make me feel good and special that he cared about me and wanted to protect me, but now that we were both into our twenties, I just wished he'd let up a bit. How would I ever find a boyfriend with Asher's daunting threats forever fresh on every male's mind this side of the bay bridge? You'd almost think that Ash wanted me for himself, but I knew that would never happen. His feelings for me were strong, as strong as mine for him, but his were more of a sister/brother pull that kept us close, not the physical attraction mine were.

"Hi, Ash," Lisa Stone sidled up against Ash's arm. "So sorry about your mom. Let me know if I can do anything for you, okay?"

"Thanks," Ash responded and eyed me over the edge of his cup as he took a sip.

"Hi, Mel. Heard you two playing in the courtyard earlier. You are so good," she said, placing her hand upon

Ash's shoulder. "When are you performing again at the Tank?"

"Tomorrow night," Ash supplied.

"I'll be there. See you then." She turned and headed toward a table in the back where a small group of men and women were gathered.

I turned in the other direction, not wanting to watch Ash's gaze follow Lisa's rear end.

"What?" he said when he finally glanced back at me.

"Nothing," I said, rolling my eyes.

"Don't give me that, 'nothing,' Mel. She's nice."

"Sure. Whatever you say."

"What's that supposed to mean?"

"Nothing!"

"I know you better than you know yourself, Melody Grace Stevens, and when you say nothing and roll your eyes, there is definitely something."

"Okay. It just seems like she's throwing herself and her very large breasts at you all the time. It's rather embarrassing how she comes across so needy."

"Needy? I thought it was sexy."

"You would. Look, I don't care. It's none of my business who with or where you get your jollies off." If that's the type of woman Ash was attracted to, no wonder he and I had never become anything more than friends.

I turned to see Alex walk through the door. Ash stiffened and sucked up the rest of his coffee. "Are you about finished?"

"No, what's your hurry?" I asked, only halfway finished with my coffee.

I glanced back toward Alex. He wore a light grey denim shirt, the sleeves rolled up just below his elbows, showing off some cool tattoos on his forearms. The veins protruding as he reached up and swiped his hair off his forehead. He looked good. Really good. Almost as good as Ash. I quickly averted my eyes, not wanting him to know I'd been ogling him as he headed over toward us.

Ash knew Alex from way back in high school, but the few times I'd seen them both in the same room together, Ash always seemed a bit put off or uneasy.

"Hey, Melody. I've been looking for you," Alex said, putting his arm around my shoulder when he reached us. Ash looked on, frowning.

"I'm right here," I said with a slight giggle.

"I have two tickets to see Maroon Five at the Shoreline next Friday night. Wanna go?"

"Okay. Sure," I said, sucking in my bottom lip, dying inside with excitement at the prospect of a real date with a real guy. I mean someone other than Asher Beaumont. Ash and I went everywhere together, so they never seemed like dates. And they weren't, of course.

Chapter Three

Asher

I knew I had no say in whom Mel went out with, but Alex Clayton? Of all the creeps that walked this earth, why did Alex Clayton suddenly have eyes for Melody? The guy had a different woman on his arm every time I saw him come into the club. Mel was innocent and fragile. He'd only end up hurting her.

I stood watching them. Mel laughing at everything he said, which was garbage as far as I was concerned. After about five minutes of that crap, I'd had enough. I couldn't stand there and watch his ugly display of flirtation any longer.

"Mel, I gotta go. Are you coming?"

She frowned at me and gave Alex an apologetic glance. "Sorry, I need to go."

"Okay. I'll call you and let you know what time."

"Sounds good," she said, placing her unfinished coffee down on the corner of the table we'd been standing near and making an apathetic approach toward me and the door.

I let the door close after Mel had scooted through under my arm that had been holding it open. She hurried up the walkway toward the apartment that she shared with her roommate, Erica, not waiting for me or stopping when I called out to her.

"Mel. Wait! C'mon, Melody. What's your problem?"

She stopped and turned to face me. "You, you're the problem, Asher."

"What are you talking about? What did I do?"

She poked her finger into my chest. "You know perfectly well what you did." When she finished poking me, she took off again toward home.

"No, I don't. What did I do?"

She stopped abruptly and her guitar case strap fell off her shoulder and dangled on her upper arm. I took her other arm in my hand to keep her from taking off again. "For a guy who had the sweetest, kindest, most caring and intelligent mother in the whole entire world—may she rest in peace—you suddenly have the I.Q. of an orangutan."

That was harsh. Especially since we'd just spread my mom's ashes out over the bay.

"You're mad for some reason, and I don't know why."

I let go of her arm, and she sighed. "Asher, do you realize that tonight was the very first time I've ever been asked to go to a concert—or anywhere—with a guy?"

"No, it's not. You and I go places all the time and we've been to plenty of concerts."

She shook her head. "Not the same."

As if a bolt of lightning sizzled down the center of my body, I suddenly realized she'd never been on an actual date with anyone before. Though that realization was startling, I didn't see what that had to do with her being upset with me. And why did the first date she'd been asked to go on have to be with Alex Clayton? He was nothing more than a suit, a wannabe attorney, working in a Market Street law firm as an associate.

There were plenty of other guys she could go out with, guys we both knew that would treat her far better than Alex fucking Clayton. They knew I'd kick the shit out of them if they didn't.

"I'm sorry. But, what did I do that was so wrong?"

"Forget it, Ash. Let's just go home. I'm tired, and if you want my help tomorrow going through your mom's stuff, I need to get some sleep." She turned and began to walk up the hill.

"Mel, why Alex Clayton?"

She stopped. "Why not Alex?"

I ran my hand through my hair. She was making this very difficult and frustrating. "You know, he's been coming to the club for the past six or seven months now."

"Believe me, I've noticed," she said with a twinkle in her eye that I didn't like being there while she talked about Alex.

"And have you noticed that every time he comes in it's with a different woman?"

She looked at the ground then back up at me. "Sure. He works with most of them."

That was a stretch of the word "works." I didn't want to argue with her anymore, but she had to know. "Mel, he brings them in, hanging on his arm." She had to see where I was going with this.

"So?"

"Do I really need to spell it out for you?"

"I guess so, Asher because Alex has been nothing but kind and nice to me every time I've seen him."

"He's fucking them. A different one every time he comes in. I don't want you to get hurt."

She gave me a pensive look and shook her head. "I don't believe you. You're just saying all this because I gave you a hard time about Lisa and her boobs. And besides, I don't need you to worry about me. I don't tell you who you can or can't go out with."

"That's because I'm a guy."

"Really? That's your reasoning? You think you have the right to dictate my social life because you're a guy? Just leave me the fuck alone." She tugged the strap of her guitar case back up onto her shoulder and stormed off. This time, I let her go. I watched her for a few seconds, the cumbersome case bumping against her rear end as she stomped up the hill. I was tired. Too damn tired to fight, and I didn't *want* to fight, not with Mel. I did think about going back inside the bar and decorating Alex's face, though, but my exhaustion took hold. It had been a hellish day with the memorial and all. I looked forward to my pillow and closing my eyes.

I repositioned the strap of my own case on my shoulder and walked quickly up the hill, close behind Mel. She'd made me mad, but I didn't want her walking through the neighborhood alone.

When she reached the apartment building we lived in, I'd practically caught up with her. I was close enough to catch the door before it slammed shut behind her. Good thing, since I'd forgotten my key this morning.

Mel and Erica lived across the hall from me. Mel had moved in with Erica shortly after I started my lease. We'd met Erica when Mel was helping me move in. They'd hit it off right away, and lucky for Mel, Erica had recently lost her roommate and was looking for a new one.

I gave Mel some space between us and let her walk up the steps ahead of me. I heard her apartment door squeak open and then close as I reached the top step of the stairs. The brownstone consisted of four apartments, two upstairs and two on the ground floor. I got to my place and turned the handle. I never locked my apartment door. I figured with the main one downstairs always locked, I didn't really need to. I knew that Mel and Erica always locked theirs, though. The two renters downstairs were both guys a little older than us. They were friendly but kept mostly to themselves. Living in this building was more like living in a huge house, except everyone's room had a sitting room and a kitchen. So it just seemed silly to me to lock the inside door.

I placed my guitar across the sofa and headed to the kitchen for a glass of water. As I stood drinking and watching all the twinkling lights from my kitchen window that overlooked the city, I wanted to throw the glass into the sink and let it shatter into a million pieces. I hated fighting with Melody. She was right, though, I didn't have any right to tell her who she could go out with. But damn it, I just didn't like that guy. I'd spent too may nights up on stage, watching him play Don Juan with a different woman every time he was in the club. It turned my stomach to think of Mel being alone with him. She could have picked anyone else, and I'd have been fine with it. I just couldn't stand by and let her go out with Alex. But, at the same time, I didn't like this feeling I had about her and the way we were arguing about him either. I put the empty glass in the sink and headed to bed. I was beat. It had been a shitty day. I'd said goodbye to my mom forever, and then had a fight with my best friend over some creep.

Fuck.

It hit me again, then. I was alone in the world now. Spreading my mom's ashes over the bay this evening solidified that reality for me. I didn't want to lose Mel, too. My mom was gone. My mind drifted back to my dad. My *dad*, well, he'd never really been around had he? But he was gone from this world, too. There were two other people I didn't really like to think about that were still around. I'd always hated them. From the time I'd found out about them. Hated knowing they existed. I had two brothers, well, half-brothers. Fuck. My mom never talked about them, and it had been the last thing I wanted to bring up as she lay on her deathbed. And now that she was gone, I didn't have anyone left to ask about them.

I shrugged out of my clothes and sank beneath the covers on my bed. It was still fairly early, but emotional exhaustion took hold and I closed my eyes, thinking about clever ways to apologize to Mel without giving up my quest to get her to see my side about what she'd be getting herself into with Alex.

I moaned at the jiggling pressure on my shoulder.

"Wake up. Why are you in bed anyway?" Mel's urgent voice snapped into my ears, interrupting a very good dream.

"What's going on?" I asked.

"It's only nine o'clock. Why are you in bed already?"

I rubbed my eyes and looked at her all-too-perky face. "I was tired."

"Oh. Right. Sorry, today was pretty rough." She sat, making herself comfortable on the edge of my bed.

"Yeah, it was." I sat up a little, letting the covers fall to my waist, exposing my naked chest.

Mel stood up, walked to my window and stared out. "You sleep naked?" she asked.

"No, I have boxers on. Why?"

She shook her head and continued to stare out the window.

"You've seen me in swim trunks. It's basically the same thing."

"I haven't actually seen you in swim trunks for two summers. I spent most of last summer at my dad's, remember? You've changed since then."

I looked down at my torso. I guess my chest was a bit larger than it had been. I knew my arms were. Trips to the gym were now a daily routine for me. Or at least, I tried. Sometimes life…and death took precedence over bodybuilding.

"What are you doing here, Mel?" I pushed the covers off and got out of bed. She turned to face me and her eyes traveled down to my bare thighs and lingered there for a few seconds before they came back up to my face. "I thought you were mad at me."

"I was. Am. I don't want my soc—"

"Wait," I interrupted. "Listen, I know I don't have any right to tell you who you can date. It's just that, Mel, this guy, you need to understand…he's…"

"Nice to me," she supplied before I had a chance to finished. *Not* what I had intended to say.

"I get that. I'm sure he's very nice."

"Then what's your problem?"

"I meant…I'm sure he's very nice to all the women he screws. He's got a reputation for sleeping around with every woman he brings to the club. And I worry that might be all he wants from you, too." In fact, I was positive that was all he wanted.

"I can take care of myself. I'm a big girl, I don't need you to worry about me."

"Mel, those other women are so much more..." Her eyebrows lifted. I needed to be careful here. "Those other women are looking for sex. You can tell by the way they dress, dripping with sensuality."

"Maybe I am, too."

Now *my* eyebrows shot up. "Don't be ridiculous."

"What? You don't think I'm sexy?"

"I never said that." Melody Stevens had not only grown up to be sexy, but smokin' hot. "But if sex is what you're looking for, why would you pick him?"

She shrugged. Now I really wanted to pummel the asshole.

"Ash, I don't want to argue about my social life with you. We've never tried to control each other before."

I ran a hand over my tired face, trying to make some sense of what she really wanted. I didn't think we were talking about her "social" life anymore. Was she really planning to have Alex fucking Clayton be her first lay? "I'm not trying to control you. I just don't want you to get hurt."

"I promise, I won't get hurt."

"You don't know anything about sex, Mel."

Her eyes grew huge and she looked like she wanted to hit me as I realized what I'd just said.

"How the fuck would you know? she asked.

I shook my head. "I'm sorry. I meant to say...you're not as experienced as those other women."

"Too late. You already said it. I may not have had sex before, but I know what to do."

"The guy's a man whore, Melody."

"Good, then maybe he'll teach me something. And you know what, Asher? If he does, then I'll be able to tell you all the stuff you don't know about sex."

I started to laugh and caught myself. She didn't know anything about my sexual experiences with women. Having her think I didn't know anything stung a little bit, but I'd never told her about any of the women I'd been with. I'd never thought it was something she wanted or needed to know. But I wasn't going to go there. Sure, she knew I dated, knew I'd had sex, or guessed. It just wasn't something we ever discussed.

Just then, her phone sang out a silly Taylor Swift song. Something about trouble. I had to laugh. Yeah, trouble was brewing. She looked at the screen. "It's Teddy," she said, a smile forming as she put the phone to her ear and began talking. Her brother Ted had moved to Phoenix after he graduated from Arizona State. He worked in some large real estate investment firm there now. He'd received a great recommendation from one of his professors for the position.

"You're here? In the city?" Her eyes shot to mine and a broad smile graced her face. "Yeah, we can be there in twenty minutes." She rolled her eyes at me. "Ash just needs to put some clothes on his scrawny body." She chuckled and turned back to the window again. Ted must have said something insultingly humorous about me, as well because her chuckle turned into a cute little giggle that could melt the heart of any male between the ages of two and ninety. I got the hint and started to pull on my jeans. It seemed we were going out. As exhausted as I was, the prospect of seeing Ted filled me with renewed energy. He was the big brother I never had. Not that I ever wanted either of my real half-brothers in my life. They were in another universe. Non-existent to me most of the time.

"Come on, Ash, shake a leg. Teddy's in town," she squealed like a thirteen-year-old. She worshiped her big brother. I wasn't jealous about that. I sort of felt the same way about Ted. He'd always been the brother mine never were. I had to remind myself that it wasn't really their fault, though. They most likely didn't even know about me.

Maybe Teddy could talk some sense into his little sister? Though I doubted the subject of having sex with Alex Clayton would ever come up.

Chapter Four

Melody

Seeing Ash without a shirt and wearing only his boxers did bizarre, quirky things to my insides. I'd needed to focus on what was happening outside the window, which wasn't much, so I didn't stare any longer than I already had. My cheeks burned at the sight of him in all that…tight, muscley skin. I had no idea guys could change that much in just two years. I'd noticed his arms, of course, but I'd never imagined his chest could be so magnificent, and his thighs, oh my goodness…so lean, yet so taut and firm. I would have loved to run my fingertips up the light dusting of golden brown hairs covering them, just to see if they were as soft as they looked.

Thank God my brother had called and yanked me out of that stupid daydream. Crushing on Ash? He was off limits. Had always *been* off limits. When we were younger, we'd made some silly pact to marry each other when we grew up. Even at eleven years old, I'd had such a ridiculously strong crush on him that the next day I could barely even talk to him. When he never brought it up again, well, that was enough of a hint for me not to go anywhere near that notion. When we got older, I was too chicken to bring it up again for fear he'd laugh. He'd probably forgotten all about it anyway, and never once had he given me any indication that he liked me that way. A silly, childish crush. That's all it was.

Looking at him now, though, I had some of those old, tingling feelings in my stomach popping back up again.

"Come on." Ash tugged me out of his apartment and down the stairs. His voice was coated with total and complete elation at the prospect of hanging with Ted tonight. I was feeling the same way. My two best friends together again.

The wind howled, and I wished I'd insisted that we stop at my apartment so I could grab a heavier jacket before we headed out. All I had on was a zip-up hooded sweatshirt and my favorite blue and white scarf. Ash had given it to me two years ago for Christmas, and I wore it practically all the time as soon as the weather started to cool down. It was made of something called viscose rayon and polyester. It was lightweight, more for fashion, not enough to keep me warm on a chilly night like tonight. We walked quickly, and I had my arms wrapped around my chest to help ward off the breeze coming from the sea.

Ash turned to me halfway down the hill. "You're cold."

I nodded but kept walking.

"Your nose is red," he chuckled. "Come here." He put his arm around me like it was no big deal, and honestly? It wasn't. It wasn't the first time he'd tried to keep me warm.

But lately, being so close to him only made me more aware of how much I was attracted to him.

We ran and skipped down the hill towards the bar, which was no small feat with Asher's arm around me. We laughed hysterically as I lost my balance and almost did a face-plant in the gutter. But the support of Ash's strong arm held me up.

Ash held the huge door open as I slipped in under his arm and headed for the lounge area. Passing the warm fire they had blazing in the fireplace, I stopped for a moment to bask in its warmth and rub my hands together in front of it. Another pair of strong arms swooped me off my feet from behind then placed me back down. I turned to see my brother's infectious grin.

"What took you guys so long?" he asked.

"Teddy!"

He took me back into his arms and hugged me tightly to him. I was in heaven.

"God, I've missed you," he breathed into my hair and squeezed again. I felt his chin lift and he let me go. Only to embrace Ash the same way he had me. It was like I had two brothers. Except I'd never really thought of Ash as a brother. Never. I'd envisioned him as my knight in shinning armor more times than I could count, but never as my brother.

"It's great to see you, Ted. How long will you be in the city? And where are you staying? You know you could always stay with me," Asher said with hopeful eyes.

"Thanks, but I have a room at the Fairmont."

"Whoa? That's crazy!" I said. "That job must be paying you beaucoup bucks."

"That, and they're flippin' the bill, too." He laughed. "I'm here on business. We're here to analyze one of the new

28

properties that Trentco recently purchased, but I couldn't visit the city without seeing you guys."

"You better not. Ever!" I said.

"That's some business trip for them to be putting you up at the Fairmont," Ash said.

"It is. I got a promotion yesterday. This is my first day in my new position as Financial Department Head, and they sent me on a last minute trip. I'm now one step away from VP," Ted said with an air of confidence. I couldn't blame him. He'd worked hard to get where he was.

"I'm proud of you, big bro." I gave him another squeeze around the middle.

"Yeah, congratulations!" Ash said.

"Let's celebrate! Shots? What are you drinking?" I asked Ted.

"One of those pale ales they're promoting. I can't stay out too late. I have an early meeting. Then I head back to Phoenix immediately after that."

"Aw, that's not fair," I pouted.

"Sorry, Mel. This is the best I can do for a visit right now. I'll be home for Thanksgiving and then again at Christmas. The entire company shuts down for two weeks between December 21st and January 4th. I'll have two weeks to hang with you two clowns. Listen, Ash, I'm sorry about your mom. I'll miss her. She was always like a second mother to Mel and me. I peeked in at the memorial this morning, but I couldn't stay long so I snuck out. I'm sorry. I knew if you'd seen me, you would have tried to talk me into staying and it was a meeting I couldn't miss."

"I would have understood, but thanks. She loved you, too," Ash said then turned toward the bar and ordered two drafts for us.

"We sprinkled her ashes off the bridge earlier this evening. It was hard on him," I whispered close to Ted's ear.

"I wish I could have been there for him, too. He's all alone now, Mel. You need to help him through everything," he whispered back. His comment gave me a sick feeling of dread in the pit of my stomach. I wanted to ask why he'd said that. Ash had him, too. Didn't he? They were like brothers.

"You make it sound like you're not going to be around much," I said with a pout I hoped he'd catch. I didn't like not having my brother around.

"I'm in Phoenix now, Mel. I wish I could be here for you both, but if I want to get ahead, I need to be there. It won't be forever. I'll move back someday. Maybe sooner than you think," he added that last part with a warm smile and a strong arm around my shoulders, squeezing me to him.

Asher turned back around and handed me one of the pints.

"What is it?" I asked and Ash gave me a silly eye roll.

"Blue Moon. What else? It's the only thing you'll drink besides Guinness or Corona light."

That was true. I wasn't a huge beer drinker. I preferred wine more, but since Ted was drinking beer, I guessed Ash thought we should, too. I sipped. It was cold and hit the spot as if I'd been craving it all day.

We spent the next hour laughing and talking about what we would do when Christmas rolled around. Ted suggested we take a trip to Hawaii and said he would pay. Both Ash's and my eyebrows shot up in surprise.

"That would be so cool," I beamed. I had the best big brother in the world.

"I've been wanting to go, and well, I can't leave my two best friends at home. Can I?"

"No. You can't." Ash laughed. "But you're not going to pay for the whole trip. I can pay, too."

"You bet," Ted said, knowing there was no arguing about it because Ash wouldn't go if he couldn't pay. "I'll start making plans when I get back to Phoenix. There's a guy I work with who has a timeshare and he already said it was available. All we need now are plane tickets."

"This is going to be so awesome!" I squealed. Christmas with my two best friends. In Hawaii. What could be better than that?

Chapter Five

Asher

Melody, as usual, took off for the bathroom after drinking one beer. She never could drink much of the stuff before having to relieve herself. I probably should have ordered her wine, but this reunion just shouted *beer* to me.

Seeing Ted always gave me a sense of belonging. We were family, and having just spread my mom's ashes out over the bay, I needed to feel like I still belonged somewhere, with someone. My mom had been all I had except for these two. Mel and Ted's parents were good people, but they'd divorced years ago when we were kids. I never really got to know their dad well, since he'd moved to San Diego shortly after the split. But at least he hadn't completely deserted them like mine had me. Mel and Ted would always take off for a month in the summer to spend time with him, leaving me alone. I always dreaded the month of July. Every summer, that month became the loneliest time of my life and made me feel even more like the forgotten sibling I was. Last year when Mel left for the entire summer and Ted had just started his internship with the firm, I'd thought I'd go apeshit from the loneliness.

While Mel was gone to the bathroom, I figured what better time to try and get Ted's help with the Alex problem.

"Listen, Ted. There's something I want to talk to you about."

"My sister?"

"Yeah." I gave him a puzzled tilt of my head. "How'd you know that?"

"Asher, I've known you practically my entire life. Do you think I can't see what's going on with the two of you?"

"What are you talking about?"

"You and Melody. The feelings you both have for each other. It's written all over your faces. I'm glad you two are finally seeing the light and each other." He chuckled and sipped at this beer.

His statement took me completely by surprise. What look was he talking about? Maybe he'd mistaken my angst at Melody's sudden urge to want to loose her virginity to some loser and her excitement at the prospect of said urge as something else. Whatever he saw, I didn't want him to think that Mel and I had anything other than what we had. Pure friendship. Twisted, but pure. Twisted in that she told me things that girls don't usually confide in a guy. Like wanting to lose her virginity.

"We don't...have...feelings...like that," I said, very slowly, not sure why he'd even assume that Mel and I were in that kind of relationship. "We aren't seeing each other. Not that way."

"Oh? Sure could have fooled me. My bad, then."

"Why would you say that, Ted?" Had I given any indication that I wanted to be with Mel romantically? Was I sending off some sort of beacon that lit up, shouting, "she's mine!" just because I didn't think she should lose her virginity to a creep like Clayton?

"Look, Ash, you and Mel…you belong together. Everyone else sees it, why don't the two of you?"

I shook my head. "Mel and I are and always have been just friends. You know that. Besides, Mel's not my type."

"Not your type. Okay. If you say so." He smirked. "So, then, what about my sister?"

Listening to Ted reveal something as awkward as his opinion about me and his sister had me strangling on my own words. Suddenly, I didn't want to tell him about that asswipe Alex and Melody's plans to have him be her first lay. After what he'd just said, he'd probably just think I was jealous. Besides, now that I thought about it, telling Ted about Mel's virginity and her plans with Alex was probably something she'd never forgive me for. Ted was, after all, her big brother. And if I knew Ted and the way he always protected his sister, telling him she wanted to fuck some man whore like Alex Clayton wasn't going to go over well. So I decided to take a sharp right turn, so to speak.

"I'm going to let her start playing alongside me, I think," I said quickly after a brief thought. It was something I'd thought of earlier when we were playing in the street. "In the club. She's become quite good, and her voice is like silk." All of that was the truth; it just wasn't something I needed to clear with Ted. But it was something to talk about other than Alex fucking Clayton, which I now knew I couldn't bring up. "I haven't told her yet. I was going to tell her tomorrow. Just thought I'd mention it to you tonight since you're here."

"That's great. I've always thought she should be singing with you. I'm glad you've decided to let her. I'm sure she'll be thrilled."

Ted knew me too well. It wasn't that I didn't want her singing with me before. Well, let's be honest here, I *didn't* want her singing with me because I didn't want us labeled as a "couple." Not in the sense of a relationship type of couple, but a performing duet. And not for my benefit. For hers. She was good, and with the right connections, she could be well on her way to a great career and a recording contract.

"Well, I think she needs a chance to be seen, even if it is in that small club," I said, though I wasn't entirely sure that club was right for her. I wasn't convinced she'd get the exposure she needed. "She needs a break. A break out, I mean."

"Yeah, I know what you mean."

"She's good, Ted. I mean *really* good. As in, 'top of the charts' good. She needs someone bigger than me, but she's gotta start somewhere."

"Don't sell yourself short, Ash. With or without Mel beside you, you shine. And who knows, maybe you need each other more than you realize, and you know I'm not just talking about music."

"Not that again."

"My sister needs you, Ash. I can't be here to protect her anymore."

My eyes shot to his. He was back on this again? "You know I'll always look out for her. But why are you pressing this? I told you, Melody and I could never have that kind of relationship. We get along great, always have, but there's never been any intimacy between us. Sure, we kissed back in sixth grade, but after that, we knew it would never work. We both felt it and have always stayed clear of that path."

"I just want to make sure my two best friends are happy and safe. I'm in Phoenix now. I can't be here to look after her. Our dad is back east and probably could care less, and mom is, well, in a world of her own these days."

"Melody's safe with me. We have each other's backs no matter what. So just stop your worrying, man."

"Okay. I wish I could stick around for a few days so I could hear you guys."

"Me, too."

"Maybe next time."

"Maybe next time, what?" Melody said, squeezing her delicate yet curvy frame in between us. Her breasts accidentally brushed against my arm. I didn't think she noticed, but I did. She grabbed her glass from the counter and gulped down the last few drops of beer that had to be room temperature by now.

"Oh, nothing important," Ted said. "We were just talking about the next time I come see you guys, we'd be able to spend more time together, that's all."

"Like Christmas," I said.

"Yeah. Exactly," Ted affirmed. Then he put his arm around his sister and pulled her in for a squeeze. "We're gonna have a blast. Now, I need a shot," Ted proclaimed in a rather dangerous sounding tone. "Tequila!" he shouted to the bartender and held up three fingers.

When the shots arrived, we clinked our glasses together and drank. Melody grabbed one of the lime wedges and sucked it. I watched as her lips puckered, and my mind went back to sixth grade and the kiss we both pretended never happened.

Chapter Six

Melody

Asher and I sat on the floor in the middle of his mom's living room going through some of her old boxes of stuff. Thank goodness she didn't have a whole lot of stuff, and what she did have was well organized. We were just about finished. There were only two boxes left in the house. The rest had all been put on a truck and given to Goodwill. There'd been a few things Asher kept of hers, but not much, mostly pictures and a small case that held some of her jewelry.

"Mel, why can't you take my word for it, Alex is bad news for you."

I ignored his question. Or tried to. All day, Asher had seemed hell-bent on talking to me about my upcoming date with Alex. Actually, hell-bent on talking me out of it was more like it. Why couldn't he just let it go? I eyed the green clock in the shape of a frog hanging on the kitchen wall. That clock had been around as long as I could remember. I loved that clock. It made me think of Nora every afternoon after school, telling us we needed to do our homework before our mother got home from work. Nora worked evenings, and our mom worked days. They took turns watching us. "Are you going to take the frog clock?"

He glanced up at it and shook his head then continued to search through the box in front of him. We sat in silence for a few minutes then I asked. "Why do you care so much that I'm going to sleep with Alex?"

"Oh, so now you've just resigned yourself to the fact that you are definitely going to let him screw you?"

"I fail to see how it's any of your concern. You really need to get off my case about it. I'm going out with him Friday night whether you like it or not. He's taking me to a concert. A concert that I really want to go to. If we end up doing it, that's none of your business. And just so you know, if we do, you can be sure I'll spare you the details."

"He's a creep and he's only going to hurt you."

"I'll take my chances."

I was looking through another box of pictures. I found several photos of Ash, Ted, and me. A bunch more of just Ash at different stages of his childhood. One for every year at Christmas from the time Ash was an infant. I smiled at the sweet newborn picture of him. His hair so thick and dark, even back then. There was one with him and a man who I assumed was his dad. I'd never met him so I wasn't sure, but who else could it be? Asher looked to be about three or four maybe. He didn't talk about his dad often. I don't suppose he knew much about him. We'd moved next door to Ash and his mom shortly after my dad left us. We were lucky the day

Nora called and told my mom that the house next door to hers was available to rent. I think my mom had us packing our bags before she'd even hung up the phone.

"Is this your dad?" I asked, holding up the photo so he could see it.

Ash nodded and grabbed the snapshot.

"How old are you there?"

"Four, I think. This was probably the last time I ever saw him." He took out his wallet and tucked the picture inside one of the flaps. I felt bad for him. He'd never really had a chance to get to know his dad.

"I miss Teddy already," I said to change the subject. Plus, I was looking at different pictures of the three of us. I picked up another photo of Ash and studied it. I remembered the day it had been taken. It was his seventh birthday. We were both dressed as Star Wars characters. He was Luke and I was Leia. He'd been such a cute boy. I'd always thought so. He still was, but now I wouldn't call him cute. Now…I'd call him rather yummy looking. Especially the way he looked right at that moment. His black t-shirt hugged his chest and arms, showing off his sexy, taut muscles as he breathed in and out. I had to blink to stop my mind from wandering back to the vision of his bare chest that I'd seen last night. I stared at him for a bit, wondering what it was that had been capturing his attention for the past several minutes. His head was bent down, his hair falling over his forehead, his eyes intent, focused on something he was reading.

"I miss him, too," Asher said, finally. The way his brows knitted together gave his beautiful face a sour expression.

"What's that?"

He didn't look up. He didn't even acknowledge that I had asked him a question. He just stared at a piece of paper.

"Asher. What is that?"

"Huh?" He still didn't look up.

I got up, walked to where he sat, and plopped down beside him. He handed the paper to me and I began to read. It was a handwritten letter to Asher. I knew from the very first sentence that it was from Nora, his mom. It wasn't a long letter, just a couple of paragraphs. But what was contained in those two paragraphs had been enough to render my best friend speechless. Nora wanted him to find his two half-brothers. She'd supplied their addresses for Asher to go see them. It was the last few sentences of the note that choked me up.

"Asher, please, I beg you. Don't live your life as a lonely, bitter man. Find your brothers, Jackson and Brodie. You have to believe that they had nothing to do with the way your father treated you or me. Remember, he abandoned them the same way he deserted you."

I didn't say anything at first. I waited, wanting to hear something from Ash. Instead of saying something, he grabbed the letter back, crumpled it into a ball, and tossed it overhanded across the room and into the wastebasket. Normally, I would have laughed and said "good shot." Then I would have picked up another piece of paper and crumpled it too before sending it across the room to the trash. Then we'd take turns until someone lost, which was usually me.

"What are you going to do?" I said at the risk of being told to mind my own business. Asher hated those two guys, though from what Nora had told my mom, I knew they probably didn't even know Ash existed.

"Nothing. That's what I'm going to do. I don't need them, and they, sure as shit, don't need me."

I bit my lower lip. I was lucky to have Ted. But I knew that if Teddy and I ever found out we had another sibling somewhere, we'd want to meet them. Maybe get to know them. "I think you should do what your mother wanted."

"I didn't ask you." He closed up the box and stood, ready to leave. I closed the one I was looking through and stood, as well.

"No. You didn't. But I'm your best friend. And as your best friend, I'm telling you to go find them. If for no other reason than to look them in the eyes and say, 'phooey on you, assholes.'"

Ash laughed. "That's what you think I should say?"

"I don't know. Maybe. What difference does it make what you say? Nora said they didn't have anything to do with how your father treated you. I'm not saying they will embrace you, Ash, or accept you as their brother. Hell, they may hate you more than you hate them. Or maybe they won't. Maybe they'll feel lucky to have discovered another brother. I love my brother and I'm lucky I have him. I wouldn't give him up for the world. Now you have a chance to have brothers, Asher. They may or may not want you in their lives, but you'll never know unless you go find them."

He took a step toward me, closing the gap between us, and placed his hand at the nape of my neck to draw me in close, his forehead pressed against mine. I stopped breathing, unsure of what he was doing. "Ah, Melly. You have no idea what the hell you're talking about. You've never *not* had the love of your brother, *or* me. This is different."

He stepped away and grabbed his jacket from the chair he'd draped it over when we first got there. "Lock the door when you leave," he said. Without looking at me, he picked up the two boxes under one arm and walked out, closing the door behind him. I watched him through the window as he got into his car. A minute later, he was gone.

God, he was infuriating sometimes. I stood there, biting my lower lip. *What was that?* He'd never, ever, touched me that way before. And then to just leave?

Good thing I'd brought my own car or I'd be forced to spend the night at Mom's or beg her for a ride to the Bart station. Neither option was appealing. I loved my mom and I liked visiting with her, but I didn't want to sleep in my old room. It wasn't my room anymore. Not with the new yellow and white frilly curtains and bedspread she'd changed it to shortly after I moved out. I'd always kept my room dark. I liked it that way. Not morbid dark, but decorated in dark colors like red or purple. Anything vibrant that made me feel alive and not so little girlish. Maybe that was because I hung around with two larger than life guys all the time and I needed something to give myself some character.

I glanced at the small green clock shaped like a frog still hanging in the kitchen. Crap. It was four in the afternoon. I'd brought my own car because I'd planned to stop next door and visit with Mom, but it looked like that would have to be some other time. I didn't want to get caught in rush hour traffic. Except, she'd be pissed if I just left without saying hello. I grabbed the clock and then reached into the wastebasket and snatched the crumpled up letter before heading out the door. I glanced at the driveway as I headed to my car. My mom's car was gone. Good, then I wouldn't need to be delayed.

The traffic hadn't been as gnarly as I'd anticipated. In fact, I don't think it took me more than twenty minutes to get home. I pulled into my parking space and saw Asher's car in his. The bum. There I was, doing him a favor by helping him go through his mom's stuff, and he'd just taken off to come home, leaving me there. Just because I thought he should make contact with his brothers? Geesh. I loved my brother. I couldn't imagine not having him in my life.

I walked past Ash's apartment door. He'd left it slightly ajar so I peeked in. He was sitting on his sofa; his hair wet and uncombed. All he had on was a pair of basketball shorts. It looked like he'd just gotten out of the shower. A bottle of Jack Daniels stood open on the table in front of him along with two shot glasses.

I cleared my throat and he looked up at me. He didn't say anything. He didn't need to. I knew what this was. I stepped in and closed the door behind me, placing my purse over the hook on the wall next to the entry with my jacket over it. I walked to the sofa and sat next to him. He poured the whiskey to the brim of each glass and handed one to me.

This was our ritual when one of us was depressed, distraught, or frustrated. Except this time, I had to work extremely hard to keep from checking out his naked chest.

I'd actually been waiting for one of these sessions since Nora passed away. I was sort of surprised it had taken this long. We didn't clink our glasses, we just downed the contents. This wasn't a celebratory moment. It was a, "I need to get wasted" moment, so I resigned myself to the fact that I wasn't going anywhere tonight. I'd be staying in with my best friend, helping him deal with all the hell he'd been going through the past several months ever since he found out that his mom had the tumor. This wasn't the first session as a result of that subject, of course, but it was the first one since she'd left this world and her only son. So, I would sit here with him in silence until he was ready to speak.

He poured the second shot, but I didn't touch it. I knew the rules. We had to do it together, and it didn't look like Asher was ready. He just sat and stared at the two glasses for what seemed like several minutes. Finally, he sighed heavily and spoke so softly I could barely make out the words.

"I don't want you to sleep with Alex."

"What?"

Surely, I'd misheard him. That was the last thing I'd expected to leave his lips. What I had expected was, "I'm sorry for leaving you at the house" or maybe "you're right, I should go meet my brothers." Or, "I just can't stand not having my mom around anymore." Something like that. Not anything about my sex life, or lack thereof. Why was he even thinking about my sex life?

"I don't want Alex Clayton to be your first," he said.

"I...uh...you don't have any say in that, Asher. It's really none of your business."

"Yes. I. Do. And yes it is."

"Why? What gives you the right?"

He picked up his glass and waited for me to pick up mine. I knew he wouldn't answer me until we drank. So we did.

He placed his glass down.

"Because, Melody, I'm your best friend, and best friends don't let their best friends fuck idiots."

I laughed.

But Asher wasn't even smiling.

Chapter Seven

Asher

I hadn't been trying to make a joke. I was as serious as a hundred-car pileup on Hwy 101 during rush hour traffic. There had to be something I could do to make her realize the mistake she would be making. I picked up her hand, and her eyes shot to mine. The emerald pools sparkled with the glow of alcohol. I'll admit, the whiskey was beginning to take effect, but I knew how much liquor Melody could handle before she was no longer in charge of her mental faculties. Two shots were nothing. This girl could drink a two-hundred-pound linebacker under the table. I'd only seen her completely plastered once. And that was because she hadn't eaten that entire day. I knew she'd eaten today because we'd had humongous burgers at the Relish Bar just three hours ago when we took a break from clearing out my mom's house.

Tonight's little "session," as we always called them, wasn't about drinking ourselves stupid this time. Not in my mind. I didn't want to be drunk. I didn't want her to be drunk. Actually, I needed to be sober and wanted her sober. But I needed just this little edge to give me the courage to do what I knew needed to be done. I needed her here. I needed her to be in this moment with me. I needed to be with her. At that moment, I needed her on so many fucking levels. My mom's letter…it had gotten to me, I had to admit. But it wasn't the only thing eating away at my soul. I had family. I had to come to terms with that, I knew that. But Melody and Ted were family too, and I couldn't let Melody make the biggest mistake of her life without at least trying to stop her. And I was running out of time. Her date with Alex was approaching fast, and everything that Ted had said last night about Melody and me had me wondering.

I knew that making her believe I needed a "session" would keep her here as long as I wanted or needed. That's the way we rolled.

I put my hand around the neck of the bottle of Jack, but I didn't pick it up. I was stalling. She sat, waiting patiently, not saying a word because this was my show. I'd started it, and it was a rule that whoever started the session had complete say over everything for the duration of the meeting. The other person was simply there as support. Once I spoke, she could respond.

"Mel, please don't sleep with Alex."

"Asher, why can't you just let me do what I want?" she asked.

"Because I know you don't want to do that."

"Yes, I do. I want to have sex." She picked up the small throw pillow from the corner of the sofa and hugged it to her chest. "I'm twenty-one and I've never done it. I want to know what it feels like. I'm always with you when we go out, so guys never approach me. It makes it hard to find a reasonable lay when you're always looming in the background. Alex likes me and he's not afraid of you. He's all I have."

I almost didn't know what to say to that. I felt bad that she thought I was the reason that guys never asked her out. Had she really never been on a date before? Was it really because of me? I thought back. She might be right. She never went out on the nights when I had a date. She always stayed at home. I knew this because she'd always tell me about some stupid movie she'd get sucked into every time I had a date. I was her best friend and I was the one who she partied with, went to bars with, or whatever. Yeah, I guess to another guy it might seem like she and I were a couple. Keep them from approaching. Of course, that never stopped me from pursuing a beautiful woman. But maybe that was just the difference between men and women. And Melody wasn't the type to ask a man out, that was for damn sure. So, it was up to me.

"Let *me* be your first."

"What?" Her eyes grew huge and her eyebrows rose. She placed the pillow back down beside her.

I cleared my throat. I hadn't realized those five little words would create a lump in my throat. The prospect of her *not* wanting me hadn't occurred until that very moment.

"I said, let me be your first," I repeated suddenly, feeling like a fool for even asking. Her first experience with sex should be with someone she loved, or at least someone she thought she loved or liked a lot. In a romantic way. Not me. But I cared a lot for Melody, and I could take care of her and make sure her first time was wonderful.

She placed her hand around the neck of the bottle of whiskey to pick it up, but I stopped her by wrapping my hand around her wrist.

"No more."

"I think I'm going to need one more shot because I thought you just said you wanted to have sex with me."

"I did. But I want you sober. You're going to want to remember your first time."

"But, Asher. Oh my God. Really? You want to have sex with me?"

Before I realized it, my hand was behind her head again, the same way it had been that afternoon. God, I'd been very tempted then to do what my mind and body wanted to do right now, but we'd been in the wrong place. Standing in the living room of my mother's house was not the right environment. I tugged her close now, and instead of resting my forehead against hers, my mouth pressed against her beautiful heart-shaped lips. When her lips parted out of what was most likely pure astonishment, I slipped my tongue through and let the sweet taste of whiskey mingle against our tongues. It wasn't until that very moment that I realized how much I'd been aching to kiss her. She didn't stop me like I'd thought she might; instead, she moaned into my mouth. I couldn't help the smile that graced my face as I continued to kiss her.

She'd actually moaned during the kiss. I kissed her gently then stared into her eyes for some sign that she was on board with this.

"Asher?"

"It's not your turn to talk," I said, trying to stick to the rules of our session. When she opened her mouth to protest, I silenced her with another kiss.

This time, she palmed my chest while her other hand barely touched the side of my waist. She kept her hands still, as if she were afraid to move them.

I reluctantly eased away, but held her gaze with mine, palming her cheeks so she couldn't look away. That kiss had been explosive, and I had to take a moment to adjust my train of thought.

"I think it's the only solution. You want to have sex for the experience. Alex will only hurt you. He'll fuck you one night and flaunt someone else in your face the next. You'll feel horrible and used. I can't let that happen. So, let me be your first. We're friends. Best friends. You know I won't hurt you. You know I care about your feelings. Care about *you*. We've been friends our entire lives. We're comfortable with each other. I know you like I know the back of my own hand. Who would be better to have sex with for your first time than me?" I let go of her, and she looked down at her hands. I was confident that I'd be able to have sex with Melody and continue our friendship. We'd never let anything like sex come between us.

"You want to have intercourse with me so that I can experience it. No other reason?"

"Yeah. No strings attached. After that, you can go out with whomever you want. I won't say a word about it."

She bit her bottom lip. Something she did whenever she was contemplating something.

"And after we do it, I go home and we pretend it never happened."

"Yeah." If that's the way she wanted it, I could do that. I'd had sex just for the pleasure of having it, knowing I'd never call or be with the woman again. I could be Mel's first and then step aside, allow her to find her true love. But I'd never be able to stand aside and let someone hurt her the way I knew someone like Alex would.

Chapter Eight

Melody

That kiss had been amazing.

Not like the kiss Asher and I had shared when we were twelve. *Nothing* like the kiss we'd shared when we were only kids. I'd been so stunned at first this time, I'd barely responded.

I was embarrassed when I moaned into his mouth and felt him smile as he kissed me. But that didn't stop him. His kiss was tender. Affectionate. So arousing.

Confusing as hell.

Especially when he'd explained further.

Could I have sex with Asher and feign indifference afterwards? As if…as if it never happened? I'd always had a secret crush on him, but I knew he didn't feel the same way about me. I'd never, in a million years, ever, *ever* imagined that Asher would *want* to have sex with me. He never had any problems getting dates, and women usually fell all over him, chomping at the bit to go to bed with him. I'd heard several women in the club bragging about him. I hated that, too. Always wishing that I were the one he'd gone home with. And here he was, offering himself to me. To use. To be my first. I'd always wanted him to be my first. Hell, I'd wanted him to be my forever, but I knew that wasn't ever going to happen. So, if I didn't take a chance, seize this moment now, I might regret it for the rest of my life—never knowing what it would have been like. But something deep down in my gut told me I shouldn't. Because it would be only once. Could I live with that? Oh God, I wanted him so bad.

"Okay," I said.

He grinned and stood up, stretching his hand out to me.

"Come with me."

I took his hand, and he led me into his bedroom. I swallowed hard when I saw the bed. It was neatly made with the top sheet and covers turned down on one side as if it was expecting us. I'm sure it probably was.

We walked to the side of the bed, and he drew me close and kissed me again. His tongue darted into my mouth, and I just melted in his arms.

Then something horrible occurred to me.

Asher, wait." I shoved him back a little. "You want to do this right now?"

"Yeah, why? What's wrong?"

"This is...completely unexpected. I'm...I'm not prepared."

"What do you need to do to be prepared?" he asked as he kissed and nibbled my neck. I thought about what I'd want to do if I had the time to get ready. I'd shower, shave my legs and armpits. Yeah, I'd definitely shave. "Can I take a shower first?"

He grinned that sexy lopsided smile of his that I'd always wanted to smother my mouth over. "Sure. Can I join you? I mean, if you want me to."

"Um…" Did I? He'd never seen me naked before, and I'd never seen him completely naked. If we were going to have sex, we'd need to be naked, right? And he would see me and I would, oh gosh, see him—something I'd only fantasized about until now. "Okay," I squeaked out the word.

He took me into his bathroom and I stood still, unsure of what to do, or how to act. He turned the faucet on then turned to me. "I'm going to undress you now."

"Okay."

His fingers slipped under the hem of my sweater and slowly lifted it up and over my head. I stood there in my bra and jeans. He'd seen me in a bathing suit before, but somehow, this was far more revealing, even though less of me was exposed now than it would have been if I were standing there in my bikini. My arms shot up to my breasts and covered my plain white bra. I suddenly wished I'd worn one of my lacy, demi-bras. I had a pink one, a pale blue one—my favorite—even a black one. But no, this morning I'd chosen to wear the most boring underwear I owned. I'd had no idea I'd be showing it to anyone, let alone Asher.

He glanced down at my feet. I still had my Converse on and I quickly kicked them off.

This moment, this act, was so different than our normal friendship. I let Asher take complete control and submitted to everything he suggested. After all, he was the one with all the experience. He left my bra fastened and undid the button on my jeans then pulled the zipper down before shoving them to my ankles.

"Hold on to me and lift your foot," he said.

I placed my hand on his shoulder and raised my left foot, slipping it out of the pant leg. Then I picked up my other foot, and he freed me of my jeans. Then he did something completely unexpected. He gently pressed his lips against the inside of my right ankle and slowly trailed little kisses up my leg and inner thigh all the way to the bottom of my ugly, plain white underpants. The sensation had my heart beating so fast I thought it would leap out of my chest, and I held my breath, thinking maybe that would stop the pounding, but it didn't. Then he stood up and brushed his lips over my mouth, his knuckles gently skimming down my cheek.

"Relax," he said in a soft, assuring tone, but I felt my body shiver with anticipation. Or was that fear? I wasn't sure. But having him undress me this way was a fantasy I'd played over and over in my head so many times I'd lost count. To be experiencing it for real was beyond my wildest imagination. Truly more spectacular than my mind had ever conjured.

He reached behind me while he kissed me and unfastened the hooks on my bra, but the pressure of our chests against each other kept it in place until he stopped kissing me and took a step backwards, pulling each strap down my arms as he retreated. His gorgeous green eyes traveled to my breasts. I pressed my lids closed, not wanting to see his expression.

"Open your eyes, Mel," he demanded. When I did, I realized that he was smiling; he licked his lips as he looked at my breasts. Then his eyes went to my ugly panties as his fingers slipped into the elastic and tugged them down to the floor. I stepped out of them the same way I'd stepped out of my pants, one foot at a time, fully aware that I now stood in front of him completely naked. His eyes met mine then traveled down to my breasts, then lower, to the light brown patch of hair between my legs. "You're perfect, Melody. Beautiful. I've always thought so, you know." I didn't know if he was waiting for me to respond or not, but I couldn't. Just the mere thought of Asher thinking about me that way sent shivers down my spine and tingles to my stomach.

He pulled his shorts down, exposing his…very large cock. I…it looked large to me at least. I wasn't a complete ignoramus. I mean, I've been on the internet. I knew what a guy looked like, and I had to say, none of them were as well endowed and as perfect as the one standing in front of me.

"Don't worry, it won't kill you." He chuckled. He must have mistaken the amazed look in my eyes at the sight of him as fear.

"No?" I joked. "But it is supposed to hurt the first time."

"We'll worry about that later. The water is warm now." He opened the shower door and took my hand as I stepped inside. The warm spray felt good. I didn't want to get my hair wet because it would take forever to dry, and I didn't want Asher to change his mind if he had to wait for me to dry my hair after the shower. But then he stepped behind me, grabbed the soap and ran it across my breasts, following each movement of the soap with his other hand, touching first my breasts, trailing down to my belly button, lathering me up with suds. When his fingers reached the top part of my mound, my stomach tingled. It was a good thing he stood behind me. I wasn't so sure I could handle looking at him naked without my knees buckling from his touch. But that thought vanished when he put his finger under my chin and prompted me to turn my head to the side. He kissed me then, and I felt powerless in his grasp as he kept my back against his chest and his hands soaped my breasts some more.

As we kissed, he turned us so that we both stood directly under the spray and all thoughts of dry hair vanished as his fingers trailed down between my legs and flowed into my folds. Having *him* touch me there was so much more satisfying than when I did it. Asher's fingers teased the area, rubbing the outside until his finger found and covered my clitoris. He moved it around, circling it, pressing it. I closed my eyes again as the sensations took hold and my mind began to float, basking in the pleasure. I gasped when two of his fingers darted inside and he flicked them rapidly for several minutes while his thumb circled my clit. He slowly eased the digits back out, coating me with my own juices. My knees collapsed and I lost my balance. He caught me and held me up as he stuck one of those fingers in his mouth, sucking off my cream. "Mmmm…Melody, you taste divine."

Oh. My. God. Did he really just do that?

Then he rubbed his other finger over my bottom lip, and I couldn't help but taste the essence of myself. He reached up and turned off the shower, grabbed the towel that hung on the hook, and dried me off, blotting my wet hair with the terry cloth so that the strands weren't dripping too much. It was going to get anything I laid on top of drenched regardless, but he didn't seem too concerned about it. I watched as he rubbed another towel over his body, his eyes intent and focused on mine. We stepped out of the shower stall and he picked me up. "Wrap your legs around me." I did as he asked, and as my legs circled his naked waist, I felt the wetness he'd created slick against his stomach. He held me tightly with his hands on my bottom as he carried me to the bed. I don't think I could have asked for a better first experience. This was turning out better than I had ever imagined.

"I'm on the pill," I blurted out, not wanting him to ask. I remembered telling him when I'd first gone on them. I know that's not something a girl usually tells a guy, but Asher was my best friend—my only friend—and I told him just about everything. I'd been unsure about whether I should go on them or not, considering I wasn't sexually active, and I'd worried what the doctor would think when I asked about them. Ash assured me that being on the pill didn't make me a slut or anything, just responsible, and that the doctor was probably used to prescribing them to women my age. But I wasn't sure if he remembered us having the discussion or not, so I thought it was important to let him know.

"I know," he said. "You told me when you first started them."

Asher kissed me as though he couldn't get enough of me, our tongues doing a crazy mating dance with a tremendous amount of fervor.

He eased me down on the bed and positioned himself on his knees over me with my legs still wrapped happily around him. I didn't want to move. Just the idea of my legs caressing his naked body was enough. I could have died a happy girl at that moment, even if we didn't go any further. Though my body had other ideas, and as he kissed his way down to my breasts, sucking a little at each nipple, teasing, nibbling, I couldn't think of anything but the fact that I wanted him inside of me. The brief moment of having his fingers inside during the shower was only a tease as to what pleasures I imagined awaited me now.

When he lowered his head and his mouth reached my belly button, I unlocked my legs from around him, and his hand slipped down between my thighs. Like before, his thumb circled my clit and his fingers slipped inside. My knees fell open and I bucked my hips; I couldn't control them as his fingers danced and strummed as though they played some sort of tune on the strings of a guitar.

Then his tongue took the place of his thumb and he flicked it and sucked at my nub until I thought I would explode into a thousand tiny pieces. The roar in my head was so strong and powerful. Then he stopped and kissed his way back up to my belly button.

"So slippery, so wet, so ready," he said.

He pulled his fingers out and positioned himself above me, one knee on each side of my thighs.

"Fuck, Mel. You are a beautiful surprise," he huffed in my ear. "I don't think I can wait any longer. I'm going to fuck you now."

He rubbed the head of his cock over my clit, and then, all of a sudden, the tip of him slipped inside of me. His movements were slow at first, but then he went all the way in. I felt a pinch, nothing more than a tiny pinprick, but the uncomfortable sensation disappeared almost immediately and became something I'd never imagined as he pulled out and pushed back in, out and in. I think I saw lightning strike across the ceiling.

Chapter Nine

Asher

Right before I plunged into Mel, I'd been overwhelmed with desire for her and I needed to be inside of her. The way she seemed so receptive to everything I suggested had me completely undone. Almost as if the primal need to claim her as mine was not only a necessity for me, but also my right. *She belonged to me.*

I'd wanted to take it slow, make the experience last. I was her first. She deserved the best I could give. During the first initial plunge, a small gasp escaped from her and her body jolted. I didn't think she even realized she'd made a sound. I eased out a little then pushed back in slowly and watched her face as the tiny lines in her forehead creased more and more with each stroke and her eyes remained tightly closed as if she were afraid to open them.

"Open your eyes, Mel. I want to see your eyes."

She blinked her baby blues wide open and our gazes held. God, she was beautiful with her blonde hair splayed all over my pillow. It was such a contrast to the dark blue color of my satin sheets.

She moaned as I pumped in a little faster. Her hands were on my rear and she tugged me in. Oh God, she was amazing. I grabbed underneath her, raising her up so that she sat facing me. I knew she felt the difference in the way I fit inside of her and she gasped at the sensation of my cock hitting her G-spot. With my hands on her hips, I edged her back and forth. I held her gaze with mine and watched as her eyes dilated with pleasure. I'd never realized how good it would feel to make love to Melody. I didn't know how I was going to feel after this was over. I needed to suppress those feelings of her belonging to me. Though, at the moment, I couldn't comprehend what that would be like. I could only concentrate on her and the experience she was having. I needed her to feel not just good, but miraculous. Because if I couldn't have her forever, then at least I'd always have this moment now of being her first and the one she would remember forever. I would always be her first, no matter what. And maybe, just maybe, she would always look back on this moment with a smile.

I slowly inched back, using my stomach muscles to hold both her and me as she stayed sitting on top of me.

"Bend your knees," I said. She did, allowing herself to kneel as she sank down on top of me. This provided her with another angle and she moaned with pleasure as my cock went deep inside. I pressed her hips back and forth as she bucked them up and down on top of me as I lifted my own hips to meet hers. Then I placed my thumb back on her clit, flicking and rubbing. When she gasped and shivered from head to toe, I knew she'd had her first orgasm. When I was sure she'd come three times, I let myself go and my climax spurted into her.

She sank down on top of me and I pivoted her so that we lay face to face on our sides. My cock still inside of her, I pulled her close against me.

"Are you okay?" I asked, my breath still ragged and huffy.

"Yes. Are you?" she breathed.

"Don't worry about me. I couldn't be better. I just want to make sure you aren't disappointed."

"Disappointment is the furthest thing from my mind."

I sighed and slowly pulled out of her, leaving the warmth of her luscious den of decadence. If my dick had a voice, it would have yelled for me to stop and stay inside of her forever.

"Don't let this change our friendship, Mel." I didn't think I would be able to live if I lost her. I didn't know how I was going to survive the rest of my life knowing she'd soon be sleeping with someone else. I was just a pawn, that's all I was. I had to keep reminding myself of that. Melody was too good for me, and her brother would kick my ass to Alaska if he ever found out what we'd just done and why. He might have his opinion that we'd make a great couple, but I doubted he'd be on board with me just letting Mel use me for the sexual experience.

"It won't. But I think we should keep this to ourselves."

"Right, if your brother ever found out…" I couldn't finish the statement at the thought of how many different ways Ted would kill me. He may have hinted that Mel and I should be together, but I knew he'd blow his stack if he ever discovered the truth about our tryst.

"It will be our little secret," she said and giggled.

"What's so funny?"

"We're fuck-buddies now."

"Is that so?"

"Well, just this once, anyway."

My gut tightened at the *just this once*. I thought I'd been prepared. Then desire ignited inside as she snuggled closer against me. A streaming trail of need followed by want confused the hell out of me.

"Asher?" she said into my chest, her lips forming a smile.

"Yeah?"

"You're hard again."

I knew that.

"Do you want to do it again?" she asked.

I glanced down at her. Surprised. No, shocked as shit would be a more apt description as she wrapped her palm around my cock. I let out a small growl and flipped her over so that my legs straddled hers.

"I suppose we should. That way you can experience what it feels like to fuck without being a virgin."

"So, the more I do it, the more I'll like it?"

"Something like that."

"I already like it," she said, splaying her hand across my chest.

"But you really should be careful who you choose." God, my mind was having a hard time with the thought of her doing it with anyone but me.

"Right now, I choose you." She lifted herself up to me and I came back down as my cock slid inside. Her soft, tight walls caressed me.

With her hands gripping my ass, she moved in circles under me. "Oh, baby, you're a quick learner."

"I have a great teacher."

Chapter Ten

Melody

I woke up in Asher's arms. We'd made love three times. After the last time, we'd both fallen asleep. I decided to call it "making love" in my mind and not just fucking. The word fucking sounded sexy when Asher said it, but for me, this time with him was more than just fucking. It was more than just sex. It would be forever ingrained in my mind as the most wonderful experience of my life. Asher would always be my first love. Always had been, always would be. No matter how many other guys I might be with in the future. I glanced at the clock on my phone. It was six thirty-two in the morning. If we didn't want anyone to find out about us, I needed to go home.

I quietly shoved the covers aside, got out of the bed, and tiptoed to the bathroom. I picked up my clothes that lay piled on the floor and quickly got dressed. I would need to sneak into my apartment. I didn't want to wake Erica. I didn't want her to know I'd been with Asher. We were roommates, but that's about as far as our friendship went. We weren't that compatible. I liked sushi; she didn't, and would always make a face whenever I brought it home. I enjoyed action movies; she wanted sappy love stories. I was fairly neat and liked a clean apartment, but she was a neat freak and always complained about stupid little things like the dishtowel not being properly hung on the hook. Hell, if it made it to the hook, I was a happy camper. Who cared if one side was longer than the other?

This wasn't the first time I'd ever fallen asleep at Ash's place while watching a movie or something, but I'd always stayed on the couch. This time, I was afraid I wouldn't be able to hide the fact that I'd slept *with* Asher. Though sleeping only took up a small fraction of what we'd actually done. I came out of the bathroom and he was still asleep so I headed out to the living room and out the front door, closing it softly behind me until it latched.

I pulled my key out of my pocket and quickly unlocked my apartment door. I went straight to my bed and climbed in. Clothes and all.

God, I'd had sex with Ash.

Yanking the covers up to my chin and burying my face into my pillow, I smiled and reflected on the night we'd spent together.

As much as we'd talked about nothing changing between us, that we'd always be best friends, something had changed tonight, and I feared that Ash and I would never be the same. I would always look at him differently. I'd always know how it felt when he kissed me. I'd always know how it felt to have him move inside of me. And I'd always know how wonderful it felt when we climaxed together. And I'd always wonder if he thought of us and what we'd done when he looked at me; if he thought of me the same way I was thinking of him. He'd never be just my friend. He would forever be my first love.

Then I cried.

Chapter Eleven

Asher

I heard Mel in the bathroom and guessed she was getting dressed to leave and go back to her own apartment. I would have given my right nut to have her come back into my bed with me, but I knew that was wrong so I feigned sleep, listened and waited for her to leave. When I heard the door shut, I sat up. What a mind fuck I'd created.

Mel had been the best thing in my life, and now I wondered if we'd ever be the same. Did we ruin everything? I knew I'd never look at her quite the same way again. I'd always be seeing her under me or on top of me. I'd always see her face as she enjoyed her first orgasm, her second and her third. I'd remember for the rest of my life how she moaned with pleasure every time I sank deep inside of her.

I was an ass.

I should have just left it alone. Let her go out with Alex and get hurt. But I couldn't bear it. I knew if he hurt her I'd be the one to hold her afterwards, but I couldn't stand the thought of him fucking her either. Not just fucking her, but being her very first. At least, this way, if she did go out with him, she'd know what it felt like to be loved during sex. Because that's what happened with me. I didn't fuck her; I'd made love to her.

I splayed my hand out over the pillow her head had rested on just a few short moments before. I pulled it to my face, inhaling the sweet scent of mango and pineapples from her hair. I closed my eyes, and as I drifted off to sleep, I tried hard to not hate myself for what I'd done.

My phone vibrated, and I opened my eyes. The time displayed on my phone read, eight seventeen. Several hours must have passed since Mel left. I swiped the on button to turn off the alarm I had permanently set on my phone. I forced myself up, and after hitting the head, I sauntered into the kitchen. I'd need a gallon of coffee this morning if I were going to do my usual five-mile run through the Presidio before going to the gym for the rest of my workout.

I thought about Mel and how beautifully sexy she'd been last night. I also thought about what she'd said about my half-brothers earlier in the day at my mom's. She'd been right, as usual. My mom wanted me to locate them so I would have family. She was sure they'd want to know about me, and was positive that they didn't already. Just one more stab of pain to my heart, knowing that my father never wanted to acknowledge me to the rest of his family. But Mel was right. I'd never know unless I made the effort to find them. But I didn't think I could do it on my own. I wanted her to come with me. But I may have ruined that.

I didn't know if we'd be able to sit in a car and be as carefree with each other as we had been before last night,

because frankly, I wanted another taste of that lovely body of
hers.

Chapter Twelve

Melody

"When did your brother say he would be home?" my mom asked as she emptied her dishwasher.

I sat in her kitchen at the small wooden table we used to have dinner on every night. I'd driven out to see her since I hadn't had a chance to stop in yesterday.

"Thanksgiving," I said, keeping my eyes set on the flowered cup filled with hot herbal tea in front of me. My fingers twirled the small fringe of my scarf. I'd put it on that morning out of habit and I was glad I had. It made Asher feel closer somehow. Though I knew that was silly. I hadn't seen Asher since we'd had sex last night. He'd gone out this morning before I'd even gotten out of bed. Running most likely. I knew he would. It was his thing. He always said he didn't get the body he had by sleeping in and lounging around all day. Now I knew first-hand just what that gorgeous body felt like on top of me and under me. I wondered what he'd thought when he woke up and found me gone.

"Well, I can't wait to see him. Life just isn't the same since he moved to Phoenix." She turned toward me after putting some cups away and fell silent for a few seconds as she stared at me. "What did you do differently?"

"Huh?"

"You look different. Did you do something with your hair?"

"No."

"Well, something is different. You look…grown-up…or something. Who's the boy?"

"What?"

"Who's the boy who has you looking so dreamily into your tea?"

I'd been thinking about Asher and the awesome, mind-blowing sex we'd had last night, but I couldn't tell her about that. And, why had she even asked? Did I have some message written on my forehead that said, "Just had my first fuck?" or "No longer a virgin?"

"I have a date tonight," I finally blurted out. Good thing it was still true…though, I wasn't as excited about it as I had been before…Asher. Shit, was I going to compare everything that happened to me now with "before Asher?"

"A date? Why didn't you tell me? What's his name, and where are you going?"

"This is why I didn't tell you. The twenty questions."

"Oh, come on, Melody. I'm your mother and I have a right to know the name of the boy you have a date with."

"Alex Clayton. And he's not a boy, he's a man."

"Okay. Well, since he's a *man*, are you still on the pill?"

"Mom!" God, she was blunt and nosy.

"I'm just asking. I know you haven't dated before, and I want you to be prepared that's all."

"I'm not thirteen. And really, Mom, I don't know which is worse, you asking me if I am still on the pill or the thought that you are actually condoning the reasons one might need to be on the pill."

"I'm not condoning sexual activity. I just want you to be cautious. That's all. You're an adult now, and well, you don't have a lot of experience."

"Now see, Mom? That's the key word here, 'adult.' I am an adult."

"Yes, you are. But I still worry, and you are still my child. No matter how old you are. Capisce?"

I reached out to grab my tea and knocked the cup over instead, spilling lukewarm tea that was sure to make a huge, ugly stain all over Mom's linen placemat.

"Sorry, Mom."

All this talk about sex had me flustered and I couldn't help wish it were Asher we were talking about, not Alex. "Don't worry about it. I'll just throw it in the washer with some bleach. It will come out. So, where is he taking you?"

"To the Maroon Five concert at the Shoreline."

"Isn't that where we went with Ted and Asher for the Bridge School concert a few years ago? We had such a great time on the lawn. Will you be on the lawn or in the seats?"

"I don't know. He didn't say." That was a good question, but I figured I'd be safe wearing jeans no matter where we sat.

"Well, be sure to take a warm jacket, honey. You know how cold the peninsula can get at night, especially this time of year."

"Yeah, I know. I should get going if I'm going get home in time to shower and change. And I don't want to get caught in rush hour traffic."

I had three hours, but still, by the time I got home, it would be close to five, and I needed a shower. I'd left this morning without taking one because I hadn't wanted to wash any remnants of Asher off me. I know that might sound nasty to some, but knowing it would be the only time we ever made love…I just couldn't bring myself to remove the smell of him. Not yet.

I wanted to take my time, sit in the tub and shave my legs, curl my hair. I wasn't sure what to expect on this date. I was excited about seeing Adam Levine, but I couldn't stop the jitters from exploding inside me at the prospect of what might happen after the concert. Would Alex be as good as Asher was? Crap, there I went again. Would I always be comparing every man I slept with to Asher? I hadn't considered that before. I bet Ash had known that would happen.

I kissed my mom goodbye and took off in my car.

I was lucky not to hit any traffic, and when I got home, I hurried up the stairs, passing Asher's open door. I couldn't help but peek in. There he was, sitting on his sofa, beer in hand and a football game on the TV.

"Hey," I said.

He looked up. "Hey. You just getting in?"

"Yeah, I was at my mom's. I gotta go."

"Wait. Where are you going?" He set his beer down on the coffee table in front of him.

"I need to get ready. I have a date with Alex, remember?"

"You're still going?" The incredulous look on his face made me mad. What did he expect? He'd said we would only be together that one time. He'd made up the rules. I had no choice but to live with them, and I had already made this date. It wasn't my problem that he didn't like Alex.

"Yeah."

"I just thought that since...well, you know. I thought you might change your mind and not go. You're not a virgin anymore so why go out with him?"

"It's Maroon Five, Ash, and I never said that. You said you didn't want Alex to be my first. And now he won't be."

"I still don't think you should sleep with him."

"Why, Asher? Why shouldn't I sleep with him? Give me a good reason."

"He'll hurt you."

"I'm a big girl. I can handle it. You can't tell me who I can and can't fuck." I turned and took off to my apartment, not waiting for his response. Last night had been nothing more than fucking to him, and I didn't want to stand in the hallway discussing my sex life.

I took a quick shower and quickly shaved my legs and underarms. I'd lost my mood for soaking in the tub. Asher made me mad as hell. He had no right to tell me that I shouldn't go out with Alex. There was only one way I'd ever allow a guy—even Asher—to dictate whom my sexual partners might be. And that was if we were in a real loving relationship. And Asher and I definitely weren't. He'd made that totally clear last night before we had sex. I couldn't even think of it as making love anymore, because it wasn't. I knew that now. That fantasy was over. It had been fucking. That's all.

Just as I was putting the finishing touches on my makeup, there was a knock at the door. I opened it to find Alex standing there. A broad smile on his handsome face turned to a semi-frown when he noticed the mascara tube in my hand. He was fifteen minutes early.

"Oh. You're not ready yet. Sorry, but I thought I'd better come a few minutes early. I heard there was an accident on the freeway."

"Okay. I'm ready enough. Just let me get my coat." I set the tube of makeup on the bathroom counter and adjusted my thong underwear, the underwear I should have been wearing last night. God, no wonder Ash only wanted that one time. I'd been wearing ugly, white, granny panties. I grabbed my coat from the hook and as I turned to lock my door, I heard Asher's apartment door open. He walked out into the hall. Perfect timing. I bet he planned it.

"Hey, Ash, what's up?" Alex gave Ash a nod.

"Nada. Mel, I'm glad I caught you. I'm gonna need your help tomorrow getting the rest of my mom's stuff together."

"Sure. What time?"

"Early. Around six."

"Six? Why do you need to go that early?"

"I just do. I have a busy day tomorrow. So, I'll wake you up sometime before that. I assume you'll be home?" This he asked while giving Alex the evil eye.

"She'll be home," Alex said and chuckled. What did he find so amusing?

"Just checking," Ash said. "Mel, don't you think you should wear something warmer? It gets really cold at the shoreline at night."

My hand went to my bare neck and exposed cleavage. I wasn't wearing Ash's scarf. I'd thought about grabbing it last minute but reconsidered, not wanting to wear something that reminded me of Ash while on my date with Alex.

"She'll be okay. I'll keep her warm," Alex grinned. "We'd better get going or we'll miss the first few songs." Alex put his arm around me and ushered me toward the steps. I wanted to pound Ash for stalling us. He knew perfectly well I wasn't planning to be home in the morning. That was if everything went the way it was supposed to go.

"Mel," Ash called out to me as I took my first step down the stairs. I turned to look at him. "Don't do it," he said.

I lowered my eyes, not wanting to see him standing there, watching me leave. He looked so dejected. But why? I knew he cared about me as his friend, but really, he needed to either deal with the fact that I needed to experience other guys, or take me in his arms and profess his undying love for me. And I knew that was never going to happen. Not in this universe.

Alex kept his arm around me as we headed down the stairs.

"What's he talking about?" Alex asked.

"Nothing important."

"He sure made it seem important."

"It's nothing. Really. He just worries about smoking weed at concerts and wants to make sure I don't," I supplied and smiled at my quick thinking.

"He doesn't need to worry about that. I don't smoke, but we *can* drink, and if he's worried about me drinking and driving, I have a surprise for you." As he held the outside door leading to the sidewalk open, I walked through, my eyes widening in amazement at the sight of the limo parked at the curb, complete with the driver standing by its open door. "Our ride," Alex grinned as he splayed his hand out toward the black, shiny car.

"A limo? Yeah, I guess there's no worries about driving."

"It's the only way to go to a concert. No parking to worry about, and no worries about getting home."

Classy, I thought and shook my head at all the bad things Ash had said about Alex. Boy was he wrong.

We sipped champagne on the way to the Shoreline and nibbled on crackers and cheese. It was a good thing he'd thought to bring something to eat since I'd forgotten all about food before leaving.

Alex and I ended up sitting in the "real seats" underneath the canopy. They were great, actually—two rows back from the stage. Maroon Five and Adam Levine were stupendous. They even had heaters above us so I wasn't cold at all. But it seemed like everything reminded me of Asher. I couldn't get him out of my head. Especially the way he'd stood at his door, watching us leave as if it were the last time he'd ever see me. I hated that look on his face.

"Oh, God, Alex, that was so freakintastic!" I said as we piled into the limo.

"I know. Adam's such a great performer," he agreed. "Want some more champagne?" He held up the unfinished bottle we'd started on our way to the concert.

"No. I think I've had enough." On top of the glass I'd had on the way to the show, I'd had two more glasses of wine during the concert. I wasn't in the mood to get drunk with the prospect of Asher waking me up so early, and knowing him, he was probably waiting up to see what time I came home. God, why did he have to make such a big deal out of this? Just as I had that thought, Alex leaned in and kissed me. His tongue darted in between my lips before I even had a chance to get to know how his mouth felt against mine. I pulled back a bit, but he held on so tight I couldn't break the seal. All I could think about was when Asher had kissed me the first time and how caring he'd been, how soft his lips felt, how tender and gentle he was when his tongue had entered my mouth. Alex was the complete opposite. He was hard and demanding and I wasn't ready for that.

I finally freed myself from his mouth and shoved him back. Not too hard, but enough so that I could breathe. He smiled at me. "You okay?"

"Yeah, I…ah…I just didn't expect that so quickly." I didn't know what to say. I didn't want to kiss him again. All my plans to have sex with him had vanished the minute his tongue assaulted my mouth.

"That wasn't quick. I've waited all night to kiss you." He leaned in again for another kiss, but I turned my head and his lips landed on my cheek. "Okay. Something's wrong."

"I'm sorry. Alex. I thought I wanted this. I thought…I just can't. The concert was fantastic and I thank you for taking me, but…I'm not going to sleep with you." There. I said it.

He laughed.

"What's so funny?"

"You." He sat back in the seat and lifted the bottle of champagne out of the holder, pouring some into one of the flutes. Then guzzled in down.

"Why do you find this so funny?"

"You're a virgin, aren't you?" he said matter-of-factly. I blinked.

"I…ah…"

"Forget it. You don't need to answer that. I already know."

"Why do you say that?" I was curious as to why he thought I was a virgin, not that I was going to tell him anything now.

"I knew the minute I started kissing you."

"I kiss like a virgin?"

"Yep."

"And how does a virgin kiss?"

"You know, timid. Not knowing what to do with your tongue and not a lot of feeling, as if you don't know how to react." What? Now I was pissed. How dare he say that?

"Maybe I just didn't want to be kissed. Did you ever think of that?"

"No. I don't think that's it."

"You're pretty sure of yourself."

He shrugged. "I've been with a lot of women. You've seen me around the club. Women go out with me because of my reputation. You knew that."

I did. Only because Asher had told me, but I wasn't about to tell Alex that. "I do now." I couldn't believe he was actually admitting to being a man whore.

"Oh come on, Melody. You knew what I wanted. You've been flirting and flaunting yourself at my dick ever since the first time our eyes locked. I've wanted you for a while now. We can fuck right here. I've heard it's very erotic in the back of a limo."

I blinked at the gauche way he'd said, "fuck." It wasn't sexy, not the way it was when Asher said it. "You're unbelievable."

"So, what do you say? Are we going to fuck or not?"

I was shocked at this man sitting beside me. What happened to the nice, kind guy I'd started the evening with? I shook my head. I was too dumbfounded to answer.

"So, you are a virgin?" He grinned. "It's okay, you don't need to be embarrassed."

I was appalled at how he'd mistaken my stunned stare for embarrassment.

"Everyone starts out that way. It's not like a disease or anything. You can tell me."

I finally found my voice. "You know what, Alex? I'm not even going to dignify that with a response. It's something you'll never find out." I had really wanted Asher to be wrong about Alex. "The concert was great. Thanks again for taking me, but now, I think you should just take me home." I inched away from him toward the corner of the leather bench seat. If I could have gone farther, I would have. I clutched my coat tightly closed in my fist and held it there.

"Suit yourself." He knocked on the barrier between the driver and us, and I watched the window slide open. "You can head back to North Beach."

"Will do," the driver said, and the window went back up.

"I had you pegged wrong, Mel. But you don't need to be afraid. Loosen up. I'm not going to force myself on you. I may like a variety of women, but I'm not a creep."

That was a matter of opinion. However, relief coated my mind that he wouldn't force me to do something I didn't want to do, but I couldn't relax. I wouldn't until I was back in my own apartment. Alone.

When we pulled up to my building, I reached for the door handle, but Alex was already on it. He opened the door for me, and I stepped out of the limo.

"Mel." I turned toward him. He'd stayed inside, sitting on the seat. "No hard feelings. Okay?"

I nodded and went inside. I tiptoed up the stairs, not wanting Asher to hear me come home. I didn't want him to know he'd been right about Alex all along. To my relief, I managed to get inside without him noticing. I slipped out of my coat and headed to my room. The apartment was dark, and I left it that way, finding my way to my room by the moonlight. Erica must have either been out or she had gone to bed already. I took off my clothes and hung them over a chair. I was too tired to be neat. I slipped into my purple, comfy pajama pants and pulled out a plain white t-shirt from my drawer, shrugging it over my head as I stepped into the bathroom. I washed my face and as I rubbed the towel across it to dry it, I eyed my birth control pills. Shit. I still hadn't taken the one from the morning so I popped one in my mouth and swallowed it. I'd skipped before, and my period had remained very minuscule, to the point of being non-existent, so I wasn't concerned about being a little late taking it this time.

I hopped into bed and pulled the covers up to my chin. There was a chill in the air, not only outside but also in my head as I thought about all the time I'd wasted thinking Alex was something to get excited about. I stared at the ceiling. I still couldn't believe how awful the evening had ended. I never wanted to see Alex Clayton again, except I knew I would. I knew he'd be back in the club, flaunting the next bimbo on his arm, but at least I hadn't given him what he'd wanted. I had no reason to concern myself with the way he acted going forward. I grabbed my phone to see if I had any missed calls. Not one. I was glad Asher hadn't tried to call me. I turned my phone off so I wouldn't hear it ring in the morning. I did not want to get up at six o'clock. I'm sure that was just Asher's way of saying I'd better be home and not at Alex's. Well, he needn't worry about that. If he couldn't call me in the morning, I was sure he'd take the hint and go without me. He'd never knock on the door that early knowing that he might wake up Erica.

Chapter Thirteen

Asher

My phone vibrated, buzzing loudly in my ear. I opened my eyes. It was still dark outside. I grabbed for my phone and noticed it was eleven forty-three at night. I didn't recognize the number. Who would be calling me at this hour? I thought of Mel being in trouble somewhere. I sat up, swiping the answer button and held the phone to my head.

"Hello?"

"Asher."

"Karen?" It was Mel's mom and she was crying. Oh no, something awful had happened. "What's wrong? Is Mel okay?"

"I can't reach her. She isn't answering her phone. Do you know where she is?"

"I…uh…"

"It's Teddy, Ash. The police just called me. He's...he was in an accident. They said he died," she sobbed into the phone.

I couldn't speak. My throat constricted and I couldn't utter a sound. Surely I'd misunderstood her.

"Asher? Are you there?"

"Yeah, I'm here. I..." I didn't know what to say? What she was saying just didn't compute. My other best friend was dead? "What...how...are they sure?"

"I have to go identify the body. But they're pretty positive." It was difficult to understand her through the sobs. "The police are here now and they're going to take me. Asher, Melody had a date tonight, and now I can't reach her. I'm worried about her. I need you to find her and meet me at the hospital. Down at the..." Her speech was broken and difficult to understand through her sobs.

She stopped, and a couple of seconds later a different woman spoke into the phone. "Hello. This is Detective Wilson. Mrs. Stevens is having a difficult time as I'm sure you understand. Could you meet her at the city morgue with her daughter?"

"In San Francisco?"

"Yes, sir. That's where they've taken the deceased."

"But, that's not possible. He was supposed to have gone back to Phoenix two days ago."

"I'm sorry. Mr...."

"Beaumont."

"Mr. Beaumont. I'm sorry for your loss, but we are fairly certain that the deceased is Theodore Owen Stevens. The accident took place at nine fifteen this evening on the corner of Taylor and Bush Street. A hit and run. The driver of the truck that rammed into the side of Mr. Stevens' car is unknown at this time. Please meet Mrs. Stevens on the first floor in the lobby waiting room. We will be there in about twenty minutes."

"Okay. I'll be there."

"Asher?" Karen was back on the phone. "Please find my daughter."

"I will. We'll meet you there as soon as we can. Don't worry."

The call ended, and I stared blankly at the phone through blurry eyes as I swiped the tears that dripped down my cheeks. Ted was dead?

I had to go find Mel. I dialed her cell and it went straight to voicemail. Why wasn't she answering her phone? Thoughts of her discarded in some back street alley after being forced to walk home in the middle of the fucking night without a working cell phone invaded my mind. I grabbed my jeans from the chair I'd put them on and quickly tugged them up, then shrugged into a t-shirt I quickly snatched out of my drawer. I swiped my jacket off the hook and stuck my wallet in my pocket. I grabbed my keys and hurried over to Mel's apartment. I knocked.

No one answered. I knocked again, but there was still no answer. So, I did what any concerned best friend would do and pounded my fist on the door until it slowly opened. Mel stood just inside, and Erica walked out of her room, rubbing her eyes.

"What the fuck is going on?" Erica asked. "Why are you pounding on the door so late, Asher?"

"Sorry," I said to Erica. She waved her arm and headed back to her room. Mel stood with her hand on her hip. "Mel, I need to talk to you. You weren't answering your phone."

"I turned it off so you wouldn't wake me up at six, and here you are anyway and it's not even morning yet." She waved me away and started to head back to her bedroom. "Asher, if this is about Alex, I don't want to talk to you. It's none of your business. Go home."

"It's not about Alex," I croaked out, unable to contain my pain at what I had to tell her, tears flowed down my face.

"What then?" She slowly turned to look at me. "You're crying?"

"Your mom just called me because you weren't answering your phone."

"Asher, what happened?"

"It's Ted."

Her eyes glossed over with tears before I'd even finished the sentence. God, how did I tell her? "He was in an accident. He's...I'm sorry, Mel. He didn't make it."

"What are you saying?" Her voice shook with the threat of sobs, but she held steady.

"Teddy died tonight. It was a hit and run close by that hotel he was staying at."

"No." She shook her head. "That's impossible. He went back to Phoenix. He said he had to go back. You heard him. It can't be him. They've made a mistake. Tell them they made a mistake, Asher!" she shouted, and Erica came back out from her room.

She hurried over to us and draped her arm around Mel. "Come on, sweetie. Come sit down." Erica coaxed her over to the sofa.

"No. I don't want to sit down."

"Mel, we need to go meet your mom."

"My mom?"

Erica went to the kitchen, grabbed a glass, and filled it with water from the fridge. She brought it back to me.

"Thanks." I took a much-needed sip then shoved it into Mel's hand. She took it but didn't drink.

"Your mom needs you. She needs us to meet her at the…" I didn't want to say it. "…at the place where they have him."

She didn't look at me. "This is not happening. This can't be happening."

"We need to leave now, Mel. Your mom is waiting for us."

"I'll drive," Erica said.

I gave Erica a very grateful God-have-mercy-look. "Thank you."

"Okay. We'll go, and you'll see. It's not him. It can't be him."

I wasn't about to argue with Melody. I hoped to God she was right." I helped Mel up and steered her to her room so she could get dressed. I waited at the door while she pulled on some pants and then a bra before shrugging back into the t-shirt she'd been wearing. She moved slowly, like a robot. As if someone had programmed the motions into her body. Her mind was clearly somewhere else.

Erica pulled up to the curb in front of the morgue. "I'll go park the car and wait for you in the waiting room."

I held Mel up, my arm around her waist. She hadn't said a word the entire ride over. Actually, no one spoke. We were all too stunned and sad to carry on a conversation. Even Erica knew Teddy, and I'm sure she was affected by what had happened, as well. Mel didn't cry, not completely, and it surprised me, but I guessed she hadn't accepted the fact that her brother was gone.

Mel ran to her mother, whose arms were out and ready. "Mom, they must be wrong. Teddy went back to Phoenix."

Karen swiped at her tear-stained cheeks, her eyes red and glossy. "No, baby. The police are positive it's Teddy."

"I want to see him, Mom. I need to see him. I need to show you it's not him."

"Okay, honey. We'll go in together. The three of us." Karen looked at me as she grabbed my hand, and I nodded.

We followed the officer and another man wearing a white coat into a room. It was cold and smelled of antiseptic. And death. We walked up to a table with a thick, black plastic, zippered bag that I assumed held my best friend inside it. The man looked up at us.

"Ready?"

Karen nodded, and he unzipped the bag, revealing a bruised and broken, pasty-white Ted. Mel's knees gave out and I caught her before she slid all the way to the floor. I had to grab the edge of the table to steady us both because my legs wanted to buckle along with hers. Her mom leaned in and wrapped her arms around us, holding on as we all cried.

Erica was kind and offered to drive Mel's mom home, and Karen offered to make us all something to eat. I knew she'd want the company, and Mel was borderline comatose and went or did whatever anyone told her to do, so I nodded. "That sounds great. Thanks."

As we entered her house, the phone rang. Karen hurried over to it. "Hello?...Yes, this is she." There was a long pause as she listened to whomever it was on the other end and she glanced up at us. "Yes. Thank you, Officer." She placed the phone back in the cradle. "That was the police. They arrested the person who ran in to Ted's car."

"Who was it?" I asked and waited for her to give us more information.

"His name is Brandon Drake. He fled the scene on foot

after his truck plowed into Ted. He'd been drinking. They said he's only sixteen and got scared, so he ran. After checking the registration of the truck, the police found him in his bedroom at his parent's house not too far from the accident." Karen swiped at the tears running down her cheeks. "That poor boy will have to live with that for the rest of his life."

Chapter Fourteen

Melody

"It had to rain today," Ash said. "Why does it always rain when there is a funeral?"

I shook my head as I stared at the stained glass window in the church. Of course, I couldn't see the rain through the thick, colored panes, but I knew it was out there. Pounding to the ground, reminding us what a fucked up world we lived in where we couldn't even mourn our loved ones in the comfort of a beautiful day without the sky opening up, reminding us just how vulnerable we really were. Or perhaps, as I liked to think, maybe the angels were crying along with us because my big brother had been taken from the world way before he was supposed to be.

I watched my mom bend over my brother's broken body as he lay in the casket. My dad stood beside her. I was glad he was here. I could hear Mom's sobs from where we sat in the pews.

"Teddy. My baby. Oh, Teddy, what are we going to do without you? I miss you already," she cried. My dad took out a hanky from his back pocket and wiped his own eyes. He always had a hanky in his back pocket.

I hadn't cried. Not when we went to identify his body. Not when we got home. Not today. I was just numb.

My mom turned away from the casket, and my dad ushered her out of the room.

I stood up. It was my turn. I was supposed to say goodbye. How the hell was I supposed to do that? Teddy was everything to me.

"Mel?" Asher grabbed my hand and squeezed it. "You okay?"

I nodded. I think. Maybe I shook my head. It didn't matter. There was no correct answer for what I was.

Numb.

I let go of Asher's hand and slowly made my way to the casket. The body that lay inside, the shell of what was once my brother looked like one of those wax figures in a museum, surrounded by soft white silk. Why did they put dead people in white silk? Was that something my mother ordered? He couldn't feel how soft it was, but he did look peaceful, except for the bruises on his face that you could still see through the makeup. How had he gotten those bruises? It almost looked as if he'd been beaten. They said he got them from the airbag deploying on impact. They would be cremating his body after the service was over before burying his ashes in the family plot. I knew from Nora exactly how they did it and I couldn't fathom that happening to my brother. I touched his hand and it was hard, so unnatural. My legs wobbled, and as if they vanished from my body, I sank to the floor.

I felt arms surround me. "Mel, I know it's hard. Come on, baby. It's time to go."

I had no ability to get up or command my body to move or make my mouth speak. Asher lifted me, and I went along. Every nerve in my body was void of all sensation.

I sat on the sofa at my mom's house. Friends and neighbors brought food. Asher placed a glass of something golden brown in my hand and told me to drink. I didn't know what was in it. I sniffed at it. It was some kind of alcohol that smelled like almonds.

"It's Amaretto. Something to take the edge off," he said. "I'll grab you some food."

I didn't want any food, but I couldn't get my mouth to form the word "no."

A man stood by my mom. I overheard him say he worked with Ted and how sorry he was. He'd been the one to request that Ted stay the week to finalize the last-minute details for the deal they had made with some contractors. That's why my brother had still been in the city. That's why my brother had been at that spot when the truck collided into the side of Ted's car, crushing him. That's why my brother was dead. I hated that man.

I rolled over, scrunching my pillow under my head. But turning was the wrong thing to do since the bright morning sun filtered in right at the level of my eyes. I squinted. I couldn't understand how the sun could shine and act so happy when the world surrounding me was shrouded in darkness. I'd wanted the sun yesterday when we'd had the service. I thought it would help, but seeing it now only made me angry.

It didn't matter anymore what day it was, though I was semi-cognizant of time passing, of Ash coming over to talk to me, of Erica peeking her head in every now and then, bringing me tea or whatever. I don't think I'd uttered a single syllable since the night at the morgue. Not even a whimper. I couldn't cry. My brother was dead and I couldn't cry. *I'm a horrible person.* What kind of person can't cry when they lose someone they love?

Chapter Fifteen

Asher

It had been over a week since Ted's memorial, and Melody was still pretty much a robot. She only did something when someone told her to do it. Otherwise, all she did was sit and stare. I could not get through to her. No matter what I did, she just stared into empty space. I hated that I couldn't penetrate that pretty head of hers. I'd even brought up the night we had sex and how fun it was, but it didn't seem to faze her. Maybe she had enjoyed her night with Alex more than she had with me. And I hated him even more, considering he hadn't even bothered to attend her brother's funeral. I knew he would use Mel and never call her again.

"You finished here?" some muscle asked, pointing at the weight machine I stood in front of, staring into space.

My workout was just about over. I had one more set, but I looked at him and nodded. "Yeah, go ahead." I walked toward the locker room for a shower.

After a week of observing Melody's lethargic state of mind since Teddy's funeral, I began to think of that letter my mom had written to me about my half-brothers. After I had taken a shower, I hopped on my bike and headed home. I ran up the stairs, taking two at a time, and hurried to my bookshelf. I pulled the letter out from the book I'd placed it in for safekeeping after Mel had given it back to me. I was sort of glad she'd rescued it from the trash after I'd left that day. I read the end of it again.

"Asher, please, I beg you. Don't live your life as a lonely, bitter man. Find your brothers, Jackson and Brodie. You have to believe that they had nothing to do with the way your father treated you or me. Remember, he abandoned them the same way he deserted you."

She'd spent most of her life avoiding talking about them, and now that she was gone, the subject loomed over me, festering like an infected wound. What would happen if I paid them a visit and introduced myself? Why was I resisting? I knew in my heart that they had nothing to do with my father's desertion. They'd been kids, just like I had been. We were all innocent, and all products of the same asshole, except Jackson and Brodie carried the last name legitimately. I was the bastard. My mom would hit me upside the head if she ever heard me say that. She'd always told me she'd given me his name because I deserved it. What was wrong with Becket? I would have been just as happy with that last name, maybe even happier. But she said I was a part of another family and I had a right to have the last name of the man who'd helped create me. So she'd given me both—Becket and Beaumont.

So, I had two brothers. Teddy had always been like a brother to me, but now he was gone. Gone from both Melody's and my life. Now that Teddy had been taken from us, and I was never to know the joys of what the future may have held for that relationship, I had to admit, I was a little curious about Jackson and Brodie. I wondered what I might have missed out on as a kid, having them in my life. What I might miss as an adult if I didn't seek them out.

I had a plan.

I hurried across the hall to Mel's apartment. I didn't even bother to knock. I knew Erica was at work, and Melody would probably just ignore my pounding anyway. At least, that's what had happened yesterday.

I opened the door, and there she was, sitting on the sofa. The TV was on, a rerun of That '70s Show. Mel, Teddy, and I had used to watch it every week when we were kids. I shut the door quietly then sauntered to the couch and sat beside her. She didn't acknowledge me, not that I'd expected her to. She didn't budge. Didn't even blink.

Several minutes passed as the show blared on the screen.

"I miss Teddy." She uttered it so softly it took me by surprise to hear her sweet voice again.

"Me, too."

"I hardly ever saw him this past year, so it shouldn't seem so bad, but I miss him now, knowing I'll never see him again."

I placed my hand on top of hers, and she turned into me, sobbing against my chest. I held her, tears filling my own eyes. Again. I had a feeling, knowing the way Melody held things in, that this was probably the first time she'd shed any tears for her brother. I was glad I could be with her when she did. She stopped crying and eased back, swiping her hands over her eyes.

"This is the first time I've cried since he died."

"And I'm sure it won't be the last." I smiled. "It shouldn't be. You need to cry. It's part of the healing process. That's what they say anyway. You're hurting. You feel sorrow. You're entitled to shed a few tears. Crying is your body's way of releasing some of that sorrow."

"You're right. I don't know what was wrong with me. I kept blaming myself for his death. Thinking that if I'd known he was still in the city, I could have prevented it."

"How, Mel? How would you have prevented it? You can't think that way. It wasn't anyone's fault."

"I hate that man."

"What man?"

"The man who Ted worked for."

I nodded. I understood that hatred. I was feeling the same way about him. A man I didn't even know. "You know it wasn't really his fault either," I supplied, knowing that was the correct response, though I didn't believe its validity.

"I hate the boy who crashed into him, too," she added. "But I know he's young and going to jail for a while. Plus, he'll have to live with his guilt. It's just easier to hate the man who Ted worked for because he started the chain of events."

I supposed it was better that she channeled her hatred toward a man she'd never see again.

I wrapped my arm around Mel's shoulders and drew her close to me. "You're gonna be okay, Mel."

She nodded.

I took my mom's letter out of my shirt pocket, opened it up, and placed it on the coffee table directly in front of us, pressing it on the surface to flatten out the wrinkles.

"I'm going," I said.

She glanced at me.

"Will you go with me?" I asked.

She sucked in her bottom lip and shook her head.

"Mel. I need you to go with me."

"I can't."

"Why not?"

"I miss Ted."

"I miss him, too. Mel, you can't just sit around all day, moping. Teddy wouldn't want you to spend your life that way."

"You think, by me meeting your brothers, that I might be able to accept the loss of my own," she spit out in a brusque tone. It hadn't been a question, just an accusation.

"No. That's not what this is about. This is about me honoring my mom's last request and wanting you to be there with me."

"You're a big boy, Asher. You can meet your family on your own."

"You're my family, Mel. These two guys?" I pointed at the letter. "I don't know them. But I want to, I want to at least meet them, let them know I exist. And I want them to know you, because *you* are my true family, and you mean more to me than anyone or anything."

Losing Ted was hard for me, too. I needed to know that I wasn't completely alone in this world. If Mel didn't go with me, I was afraid I'd lose her, too.

I was afraid that what we'd done two weeks ago had ruined our friendship. We hadn't had a chance to talk about it. She'd gone out with Alex, even though I'd asked her not to, even after we'd made love just the night before. It had crushed me when I'd run into them in the hallway. Then with the news of Ted dying, I hadn't had the nerve to bring any of that up to her. Not that she would have heard anything I said. But now, at least I'd gotten her attention with this.

"When are you leaving?" She sniffled. I grabbed a tissue from the table and handed it to her.

"I don't know." I thought about it for a minute and remembered the promise I'd made to Ted about having Mel join me on stage. "I have a few gigs on the schedule so I need to either wait or clear them. I think I should do at least one of them, and I think you should join me."

"Join you?"

"Yeah. I think we sound great together, and I would love to have you up there with me on a regular basis. We could be a team. Ash and Mel." She frowned at me, and I shrugged. "Or Mel and Ash, whichever one you prefer." I grinned, hoping for one in return, but she rolled her eyes.

"When's your next performance?"

"Actually, it's tomorrow night."

"Hmmm…that's kinda soon. I don't know if I'd be ready without some rehearsal time."

"You've played with me enough. You don't need any rehearsal."

"What did you have in mind to play?"

"The usual. Nothing you haven't already played with me."

She tapped her finger to her lips, and as I watched her, I thought of the way they'd felt against mine. I shook my head. *Don't go there, Asher.*

"Okay. I'll join you on stage. But I'm not going to go with you to meet your brothers."

"Then I won't go either," I said, picking up the letter and crumpling it in my hand before tossing it across the room into the trashcan.

"Ash!" She stood up, walked to the little metal can, and grabbed the letter. "God, you're such a moron." She opened it and straightened the paper the best she could before joining me back on the couch. "Here." She placed it on my lap. "Fine. I'll go with you. Just don't be such a pussy about it all."

I smiled. It was nice to have her back.

Chapter Sixteen

Melody

Sitting on stage with Ash was a bit surreal. I'd been watching him up here for the past six months, always wishing I could be up here with him. And now I was.

The club was packed, and my stomach felt a bit uneasy. I hadn't eaten much over the past several days, and Ash had made me eat a cheeseburger earlier. It was probably the first solid food I'd ingested since the horrible morning I found out about Ted. I still wasn't able to eat much, but Ash said if I didn't eat, he wouldn't let me sing. So I gave in and ate half of the burger. Now I regretted every bite because I felt as if I might lose the entire meal.

I took a deep breath. Stage fright was not something I ever thought I'd have, but I was nervous as hell.

We started out with two of my favorite songs, which made it easier on me. The first was a soft ballad; the second was a rock song. When we finished the second one, I took a sip from the bottle of water sitting next to me. I looked at Ash with a smile gracing my lips, searching for a clue as to the next song he wanted to do. He began strumming, and I stopped smiling. I didn't think I could do that song.

"Come on, Mel. You can do this," he whispered and sang the first line of Elton John's *Your Song*. I swallowed to try and dislodge the ragged rock stuck in my throat. This song had too much meaning. It was too soon, and I shook my head. How could he do this song? Wasn't it too soon for him, too? His mother had died not so long ago, and then Ted, but Ash kept on strumming the chords, waiting for me to join in. It didn't seem like he was going to back down.

I sang the first line, a bit timidly, staring at Ash the entire time. Then the second verse. By the end of the first chorus, we were singing to Teddy together. This was his song.

It was probably the most difficult thing I'd ever done, but I managed to get through it. And I felt better for it. Ash pulled me in for a hug when we finished singing it. I wondered if he realized how much his hug meant to me. How much I needed it from him. He'd been keeping his distance, and I was completely confused. He was my best friend, and yeah, he'd been around me almost constantly since Ted died, but he hadn't been close. Not like before. Before the sex.

We were well into the fourth song when my heart skipped several beats. Alex Clayton sat down at the table directly in front of me and he had some woman with him, of course. It wasn't that I was upset about that, I didn't really care who he was with, but it was just disturbing that he would sit right in front of me and stare directly into my eyes as if to say, "Fuck you, bitch. I don't need to pop your virginity." At least, that's what his stare said to me as he smirked before turning to kiss the woman briefly on her lips.

I glanced at Ash, and he was frowning at Alex. No surprise there. I knew how he felt about the jerk. I hadn't talked to Ash about what had happened between Alex and me, or should I say, what *didn't* happen. I was a bit embarrassed to admit that he'd been right, and I didn't want him gloating or saying, "I told you so."

This was the first moment I'd actually had a chance to think about Alex since the tragedy that stole my brother. But now that I saw Alex again, I was glad that I hadn't given in to him. I was actually sort of relieved that he'd revealed exactly what his true intentions were with me. He could have just lied about his feelings toward me and continued with his seduction. Told me how much he liked me, how he couldn't get me out of his head. A number of romantic lines came to mind. Not that I would have given in to him, no matter what. But he could have played the "Oh come on's," a little longer until he took me home. I had to commend him on quickly ending the date so I didn't need to keep saying no.

The song we were in the middle of ended, and I picked up my bottle of water, ready to start the next one, but was grateful when Asher spoke into the microphone.

"Thank you all for coming out on this cold night. Melody and I will be right back after a short break."

We propped our guitars against our chairs and headed backstage.

"You okay?" Ash asked.

"Yeah."

"You sure? Because I can have that asshole removed if you'd like."

"No. I'm fine. It's okay." I thought of telling Ash right then that I hadn't had sex with Alex, but for some reason, I didn't think it was any of his business and decided to keep the entire night to myself. Let him think what he wanted. He didn't care anyway. He hadn't bothered to even ask me about that night. If he cared, he would have asked.

After our short break, we went back on stage and played until ten. There was a larger band starting at ten-thirty that was more for the dancing crowd, suited more for those late-night want-to-find-someone-to-take-home-and-fuck singles. Like Alex.

"Want a shot to celebrate our first performance together?" Asher asked.

"Sure."

We strolled to the bar, and Asher ordered two shots of Patron Silver. He handed one to me.

"Thanks."

"To us," he said.

I gave him a weak smile, knowing he was talking about the performance, wishing he were talking about our relationship. Whatever it had become wasn't the same. Now it was more of an awkward, walk-on-eggshells kind of friendship, with us avoiding the sexual tension that I knew was one-sided. I dreaded the conversation about Alex.

I downed the shot the same as Asher had, but something felt horribly wrong in my stomach. I ran to the bathroom and made it just in time for the vomit to land in the toilet. God, I felt sick. I rinsed my mouth out and pressed some damp, cool, paper towels against my cheeks and forehead. The coolness felt good on my skin, and some of the pink color in my cheeks came back. I wiped the black smudges of mascara from below my eyes from the tears that came automatically while I'd been throwing up. The door to the restroom opened and two women walked in. One was the woman who had been sitting with Alex.

"I can't believe I'm finally on a date with Alex," she said to her friend as she entered one of the stalls. "He is so yummy, and the way he kisses, wow! That was by far the best kiss of my life. I hope it doesn't seem awkward tomorrow at work."

The best kiss she'd ever had? And she worked with him? Yuck. I wanted to throw up again as I listened to her go on about him. I thought about warning her of what his intentions were, but decided that might not be received as well as I would hope. And they might just think I was eavesdropping and that I should mind my own business. Besides, if she worked with Alex, then she probably already knew that he'd been making his way around, sampling all the women at the office as well as at the club. I left the bathroom, not wanting to hear any more.

"You okay?" Asher asked when I came back to find him still at the bar.

"Yeah. After not eating or drinking much over the past week, I guess my body just isn't ready for food and alcohol."

"Hi, Ash. Great performance tonight." Lisa, the one with the big boobs, sashayed up close to Asher's chest. Too close, if you asked me. She gave me a curt glance then resumed her attentions toward Ash. "What are you doing later?"

Ash smiled. I looked away. I couldn't watch. She was all over him. I wanted to shove her away. No. I wanted to shove my fist down her dainty throat. Ash whispered something back to her. I couldn't hear since the music had started up again.

Lisa smiled and walked away, winking at Asher as she did.

I felt sick. Again. I placed my hand over my stomach and cringed at the discomfort I was experiencing.

"Maybe we should go," Ash said.

"I think that would be a great idea. Did you talk to Stan about leaving yet?" I asked as we walked backstage to grab our equipment.

"Yeah. I told him I'd be gone for about a month."

"You're planning to go for that long?" I was shocked.

He nodded.

"And Stan is okay with that? I thought we'd just take a vacation, go see your brothers and then come home," I admitted as we headed for the door, our guitar cases slung over our shoulders.

"Yeah, he's good with it. I thought about taking a short vacation, but what's the point of just meeting them and leaving? I decided it would be good to just play it by ear. In case the meeting goes well and I want to stick around for a while, get to know them better. Are you under pressure to be home sooner? I have the money my mom left to live on for at least the next ten years. I think I can spend a little of it for this. I think she'd want me to."

I smiled as Ash held the passenger side door of his truck open for me. "No. I agree. I think that's a great idea." I didn't really have any reason not to stay with him for that long. I didn't have a steady job. I did temp work in different offices around the city, but none of them were any place that I'd ever wanted to pursue a permanent position. I was glad to hear Asher sound so positive about the situation. It was nice that he'd come to terms with things and wasn't so bitter about having half-brothers. Teddy's death must have affected Ash in ways that I hadn't realized, but I understood completely. Ted and Asher had been as close as brothers could be. I guess that made me somewhat like a sister, though my mind would never go there. Especially now that we'd had sex. Even if it was just that one time.

My stomach twisted in a knot. This sensation was different than pain. Suddenly, I hated the thought that I'd never be with Asher again that way. My mind visualized Lisa, and how just a few short minutes ago she'd pressed her chest up against his and breathed something into his ear, probably telling him where she'd be in about an hour. I didn't relish the idea that she'd probably be sleeping with him tonight. One last fling before he left town. No, that wasn't true. I hated it. Had to admit, ever since Ash and I'd had sex, I'd been jealous of the other women in his life. My feelings for Asher had only grown stronger since the sexual encounter, and I worried that they might not ever stop.

Chapter Seventeen

Asher

I walked Mel to her door. I wanted to caress her face between my palms and kiss the living daylights out of her. I hated that Alex had to show up at the club and ruin what would have been a perfect night. But he had to flaunt that slut in front of Mel, just as I knew he would. What an ass.

I'd taken Mel's virginity so he couldn't have it. And even though we'd agreed that it would only be that one time and only for the purpose of the sexual experience for her, I'd never want to hurt her by showing off another woman so soon afterwards. That was the big difference between Alex and me. I slept around, but I wasn't out to break any records or add another notch to the bedpost. That's what Alex had done in high school when I'd first met him. He was about a year older than me, and later, when I attended the same university for two semesters before my mom got sick, I'd been in the same fraternity house. I saw the notches on his bed, actual fucking notches. I shook my head at the memory. I'd heard him brag about every one of those notches and the girl they represented, in detail, one in particular that made me cringe. Even now. I hoped he'd changed since then and would keep his mouth shut about Mel. I didn't want her to get a slutty reputation around the club just because she'd made a mistake and let Alex screw her.

Mel unlocked her door and turned to face me. "Thanks for inviting me to sing with you tonight, Ash. It was a great experience. I wish Ted could have been there."

"Me, too. But if I know Ted, I'm sure he was there."

"You're probably right." She smiled. "What time do you want to leave for, what is it? Turtle Lake?"

"Yeah. It's about a four-hour drive. If we leave here by nine at the latest, we could stop for lunch somewhere, and then head straight to Turtle Lake. My mom told me they own a bar up there. I thought maybe we should go there first. That way, I can check them out if they're there and see what they're like. You know, before I go and ruin their lives."

"You're not going to ruin their lives, Ash. Don't think that way. I bet they'll be very grateful that you took the time and had the courage to find them. But," she grinned, "that sounds like a good plan, going to the bar first. I think I can be packed and ready by nine."

"Well, no pressure on the timestamp. We'll shoot for nine and leave when we're ready."

As much as I wanted to kiss Mel, I stepped back and headed to my own apartment. She was going with me tomorrow. I was glad about that.

I spent the rest of the night packing my bags. One less thing to do in the morning. I decided one medium-sized duffle bag and one smaller backpack would be plenty for me. I didn't need a bunch of clothes. A couple of pairs of jeans, a few t-shirts, and some long-sleeved tees. I threw in a couple of button down long-sleeved shirts, too. Just in case. Plus, I had my guitar. And I knew Melody would bring hers. Knowing her, she'd probably have another large suitcase. I grabbed the tarp out of the closet. I'd need to cover and strap everything down in the back of the truck to secure it all.

Within thirty minutes, I was all packed. I grabbed a beer out of the fridge and sank down on the sofa in front of the TV. I scrolled through the channels and found an old-time horror flick, *House of Wax*, starring Vincent Price. *Hmmm...perfect*, I thought. I loved these old movies. I sank back into the corner of my old sofa and nursed my beer.

I felt a kick on the bottom of my foot. I opened my eyes to see a very perturbed Melody standing above me with her arms crossed over her chest.

"I can't believe you." She shook her head. "You're despicable, Asher Beaumont."

I blinked. "What?" I glanced around my apartment. It was morning. "I must have fallen asleep." The TV was still on, and I looked to my left. The beer I'd started was still full and standing on the table beside me, but at least I'd had the sense to put it down before I'd fallen asleep.

"I've been waiting for thirty minutes for you. It's nine-thirty. You said you wanted to leave at nine. I've been ready since eight forty-five just in case you wanted to get an earlier start, and here you are, sleeping on your sofa. You didn't even go to bed, did you?"

"I'm sorry. I'm all packed. I just need to take a quick shower. Give me fifteen minutes. Go get some coffee, will you?"

"Sure. I'll be your damn waitress. Next time you say nine o'clock, make it nine o'clock."

"I said I was sorry. It's not like we're on a set schedule or anything. We have plenty of time. We'll get there when we get there." What the fuck was she so pissed off about?

I jumped in the shower and quickly scrubbed down, letting the warm water flow over my head to help wake me up. Why was Mel so upset about finding me on the couch? I'd fallen asleep there plenty of times, nothing new about that. But this time, I hadn't even been drunk. Passing out on the sofa was something I sometimes did after coming home from drinking or a date. I hated getting into bed without a shower after a night out, so if I wasn't in the mood to get wet, I'd fall asleep there.

Great fucking movie. I didn't remember much past the opening credits. I must have been tired. The entire week of always being on alert because of Mel's fragile state must have drained my energy. I hadn't been sure of anything that she might do while mourning Ted.

I placed my hand on the wall and let the water flow down the back of my head when I heard Mel's voice. I jumped. Startled.

"Here's your coffee."

I hadn't expected her to bring the coffee to me in here. She set the coffee down without looking at me. Acting very shy, she quickly left the room, shutting the door behind her. Why was she being so timid? She'd seen me naked before. Just a few weeks ago when we'd…had sex. I thought of her standing here with me in the shower. How soft her body had been, how firm her tits were, and suckable. How sweet she'd tasted on my fingers after I'd dipped them inside of her and then let her take a taste of herself from them.

"Asher, get a move on!" Mel's voice yelled from the other side of the door.

Fuck!

I had my cock in hand, ready to come. I hadn't had a release in days because I'd been taking care of Melody. Well, she was better now, and one thing was for sure, I needed to get laid. I should have taken Lisa up on her offer last night. But for some reason, I didn't feel like being with her. Since when did I get so choosy?

My mind drifted back to Mel. She'd been so willing to do whatever I'd suggested that night. The memory of the pleasure of sinking my dick inside of her sweet, tight canal and hearing her moan with excitement had me so completely undone, I'd had a hard time holding out long enough to give her the experience she deserved. The way she'd accepted me after the first initial pinch of losing her virginity, she'd turned into a sexy vixen with the way she moved. Circling her hips under me, bucking them up when I'd thrusted in. I closed my eyes and pumped my hand against my cock hard, managing to stifle the moan that begged to escape with the much-needed release that finally came.

I pressed my forehead against the shower wall and waited for my heartbeat and breathing to return to normal. I couldn't believe I'd just jacked off thinking about Melody. While she was right in the next room. Ted's words came rushing into my mind. *Look, Ash, you and Mel...you belong together. Everyone else sees it, why don't the two of you?* Could he have been on to something? Could Melody and I ever be in that kind of relationship? Would Ted have endorsed such a relationship? It sure seemed as if he'd been headed in that direction from what he said. I'd been blind to it all, even while he was spelling it out for me. Even after

Mel and I'd had sex together, I'd still been blind to the possibility. Mel had grown into a very sexy woman, and I'd been denying my feelings and desires for her. The question now was; would she want me? I didn't think she would, considering she'd made a big deal about experiencing other guys, too. Guys like Alex fucking Clayton.

I grabbed the towel off the hook and stepped out of the shower, ready to hit the road. This was going to be an interesting trip.

Chapter Eighteen

Melody

I hated finding Asher on the sofa this morning. God, how inconsiderate of him. I knew he'd made plans with Lisa in the bar, but did he have to act so casual about everything? He didn't need to brag about his conquest by sleeping on the sofa the night before we were leaving for a trip together. I knew what it meant when he slept on the sofa. It meant he'd had sex the night before and didn't want to get into his own sheets afterwards. He'd told me that a long time ago one night during one of our sessions. He'd told me there were usually two reasons why he'd sleep on his couch. It was either because the sheets were soiled with the so-called "wet spot," or he'd had too much to drink and just crashed on the sofa. I knew he hadn't had much to drink, not when he knew we'd be heading out the next day for a four-hour drive to meet his two brothers who I'm sure he wanted to make a good impression on.

I sat on the couch, in the opposite corner from the one Ash had slept on last night and drank my coffee, waiting for him to finish in the shower. He was taking longer than the fifteen minutes he'd promised. I felt like barging in on him and hurrying his ass up. Shit, it was his idea to leave at nine o'clock, not mine. But the thought of seeing him in the shower embarrassed me. I knew what he looked like. The firm muscles of his pecs, his hard, rippled abs, and the indented v-shape leading down to his...wonderfully, beautifully large penis.

"Are you all packed and ready?" Ash asked. I jumped, spilling coffee all over myself.

"Fuck, Asher, you made me spill my coffee. You scared the crap out of me. Now I'll need to change."

He laughed. "Sorry." He stood inside his bedroom doorway in his jeans that were zipped but unbuttoned. He was shirtless and barefoot, towel drying his hair. Sexy as hell.

I wanted to run to him, wrap my arms around him and kiss him. Then I remembered Lisa and decided that I didn't want to touch him ever, ever again. It was going to be a long trip.

"Yeah, I'm ready and packed." I pointed to the two large suitcases on wheels by the door.

"Christ, woman. We're not moving up there."

"Well, I wasn't sure what I'd need. I like to be prepared."

"Okay. Give me another five minutes and we can go."

"That will give me time to change. I'll be right back."

The ride started out sort of quiet. I was still a little pissed off that he'd had sex with Lisa the night before we were supposed to leave. I didn't mention it, and neither had he, but I felt the sting of his silence. I was beginning to think I'd made a mistake by coming along. But I wanted to be there for support. Asher was my best friend. Just because he'd helped me lose my virginity didn't mean anything. I had to remember that. Asher wasn't interested in me that way. I needed to get over this stupid crush I had on him before I ended up really getting hurt when he found that someone special he'd want to spend the rest of his life with.

We stopped at a little café for lunch. I wasn't very hungry so I just ordered a small salad and a glass of water.

"Mel, you need to eat more than just a salad. You're getting too thin."

I gave him a blank stare. "You're really going to comment on my figure?"

"No. God forbid. I'm not a fool."

I giggled. I couldn't help it.

"I'm just worried about you. You haven't been taking very good care of yourself."

"I just don't feel all that well, that's all. My stomach is still feeling queasy. It started last night, remember? Maybe that cheeseburger I ate yesterday was tainted."

"Maybe. But I think if it had been, you'd be sicker than this."

I shrugged. "How would you know? Have you ever had food poisoning?"

"Yep. Don't you remember? It was after the three of us went to the county fair back in fifth grade. I ate some chicken on a stick and puked all over the backseat of your mom's car."

I laughed. "That was gross. My mom was pretty calm about it, though. If it had been my car, I would have screamed holy hell. It took two months for that stench to go away. But I thought you just got sick because of all the whirly-rides we went on after you ate the chicken on a stick."

"Whatever. I just remember feeling like crap."

My abdomen clenched again and it felt like my stomach was in a war with my esophagus. "Please. Let's change the subject."

I drank some water and ate the crackers that came with my salad. I felt a little better. I took mini bites of lettuce and cheese, but mostly ate the croutons.

It was two more hours to Turtle Lake. I just hoped my stomach settled down for the car ride ahead of us.

A little while into the ride, Asher poked me with his finger in the side. "Wake up, we're almost there."

"Really?" I stretched and yawned. "Wow, I must have fallen into a deep sleep."

"You did. You were snoring." He laughed.

"I was not."

"Yeah. It was a cute dainty snore, but still snoring. Didn't you sleep well last night?"

"Yeah, I did. I guess. I don't know why I'm so tried. Riding in a car makes me tired, but wow, to go out completely like that is strange."

"I checked out the name of their bar and plugged it into the GPS in my phone. Could you be navigator?"

"Sure." Asher handed me his phone and I studied the route with the little green ball moving along the path. "You need to take the next left on Green Valley Parkway."

A little while later, I told him where to turn. As I watched the phone, my stomach reeled with a wave of nausea. "Asher, pull over, quick!"

He steered the truck to the right and stopped. I opened the door and leaned over, losing the little bit of lunch that I'd eaten. Asher handed me a tissue and I wiped my mouth.

"Sorry," I said. "I think looking at the phone made me carsick."

"It's okay. You must have a touch of the flu or something." He placed his hand on my forehead. "No fever, though. That's good."

Chapter Nineteen

Asher

We were around the corner from where the bar was located and I stopped the truck again. I glanced at Melody; her cheeks were flushed and she didn't look well.

"Do you want to stay in the truck while I go in?"

"No. I think I'd like to go visit their bathroom. Then maybe order a ginger ale or something."

"Okay. That sounds like a good idea. I want to go in and act like customers anyway. I don't want to tell anyone who I am right away. If anyone asks, we're on our way to Bend, Oregon."

She nodded. "Got it."

"You sure you're up for this?"

"Yeah, I'm just a little carsick, that's all. I'll be fine with some food and drink."

I pulled into the small parking lot beside the bar. It was two in the afternoon and sweet music flowed into my ears as we opened the door and entered the bar. There was a band up on stage, two women harmonizing along with four guys. They were good. Strange, I thought, that they would be performing in the middle of the day. I looked around and didn't see many customers. We headed to the bar and I pulled out a stool for Mel. The guy behind the bar walked up to us.

"What can I get you?"

"I'll take a Coke and a ginger ale for her. Where is your bathroom?" I said.

He pointed behind us. "Straight back past the stage and then left at the first door."

Mel got up and walked to the head. I watched her go. I hoped she began to feel better soon, or this trip was going to be a drag. She walked right in front of the stage, and I couldn't tear my eyes from the band. I knew just by looking at them who the two guys in front were. I didn't know which one was Jackson and which one was Brodie, but that had to be them. Their features were similar to mine, and this was their bar. I didn't know they played in a band, though. That was one point in their favor. If that *was* them.

The bartender placed the Coke in front of me and the ginger ale in front of the stool where Mel had been standing before she left. I picked up the Coke and sipped. "Hey, who's the band?" I asked the bartender.

"That's The Beaumont Brothers. The two guys in front are the leads. The one on the keyboard is Jackson, and the one on the bass is Brodie."

I turned around to watch them play. They were good. They seemed cool. I had to find a way to introduce myself.

I'd thought about a hundred different scenarios regarding what I would say when we got here, but now that I was here, all of those words sounded stupid. "Hey, I'm your brother." Or "Funny thing, I'm your half-brother." Or how about, "You're gonna laugh…" None of them seemed to work right now. I didn't think any of this was funny. I just didn't know how to approach them. At that very moment, the band stopped playing.

"They perform three nights a week," the bartender said. "Stick around and you can watch them tomorrow night."

"I might."

Just then, I felt a cold and wet nuzzle on the wrist of the hand I had braced against the seat of the barstool and turned to see a large brown dog. His droopy forehead and floppy ears were typical of a hound dog, and his wagging tail suggested he was friendly. He was a beauty.

"That's Rufus," someone said from behind me. I looked over my shoulder to see the guy who had been playing the keyboard. Jackson.

"Nice dog," I said, patting Rufus on the head. His fur was smooth to the touch, and when I stopped petting him, he plopped down on the floor at my feet. Not annoying me to pet him more like so many dogs did. I could tell he was well trained.

"He's the best. And you should stay and listen. We're not bad. Hey, Derrick, let me have a water. No ice, please." He smiled at me. "So, welcome to Turtle Lake. Are you just passing through or new to our little town?"

"Just passing through on our way to Bend, Oregon," I lied. "But I think we might hang out for a while. Take a little vacation. We aren't in any hurry."

"This is a great place to hang. I ought to know. I've been hanging here practically my whole life, give or take a few years here and there. I'm Jackson Beaumont." He stuck his hand out.

"Ash," I supplied and shook his hand.

The bartender placed a glass filled with water on the counter and Jackson picked it up, drank down the entire contents then placed the empty tumbler on the bar. Mel came out of the bathroom and sat in the stool next to me. "This is my friend, Melody. Mel, this is Jackson."

"Nice to meet you, Melody."

"Nice to meet you, too."

"You feel okay?" I asked her.

She nodded. "Better now that I'm out of the truck. We're going to have to find a hotel or something. I don't think I can ride any farther today." She played along with my little ruse very well.

"Do you know of any good places to stay in the area?" I asked.

"We have a room that we lease out," Jackson said.

"The room actually belongs to my brother, but I'm sure he's up for renting it out."

"What are you volunteering me for now, Jack?"

"This is my brother, Brodie," Jackson said then turned his attention to his brother. "Just the cottage. No one is staying in it right now, right?"

"Nope, it's vacant."

"This is Ash and Melody," Jackson said.

"Nice to meet you. That gorgeous brunette over there playing with the microphone stand is my wife, Gabrielle. You looking for a room?" Brodie glanced at me.

"Yeah. For a couple of nights."

One of the women who had been singing with the band walked over and plopped down on the stool next to Mel. "Derrick, I'm dying, water, pleeeease."

"Coming right up, darlin'."

This is my wife, Lena. Lena, meet Melody and Ash," Jackson said.

"Hi." She raised her hand in a quick wave.

"They're looking for a hotel for a couple of nights."

She laughed. "Hmmm…if there's one thing this town needs, it's a few hotels."

"Ain't that the truth," Brodie agreed. "The room we have is small, but we renovated it with new furniture and new kitchen appliances. We just installed a queen-size Murphy wall bed, too. No one's even tried it yet."

I looked at Mel. "We're uh…not…we should probably have se—"

"That sounds great," Mel said, interrupting me and giving me a don't-argue-with-me look.

"Great. The cottage sits above the garage. It hasn't had anyone in it for a long time."

"Wait a minute," I said. "You people don't even know us and you're willing to rent out your room to strangers? Is there something wrong with it or something? Haunted?"

Brodie laughed. "No, man. There aren't a lot of places in this town to stay, and it's just that my brother mentioned the room. We've learned over the years that there's really no arguing with him when it comes to helping people in need. That's just the way he is. You look like a nice guy. I'm a pretty good judge of character. So, if you want to rent the room, it's yours. A day, a week, a month. However long you need it. Besides, the only hotel in this town is the historical Turtle Lake Hotel, and I think that one *might* actually be haunted." He grinned.

He was okay, I decided. "How much is it?"

Brodie rubbed his thumb and forefinger against his chin. "$20 for the night. $100 for the week. Any longer than that, we'll tack on an additional discount for you."

That was pretty cheap. I looked at Mel and she smiled, nodding her head.

"Okay. You got a deal," I said.

"You got it."

Just then, the other woman walked up and put her arm around Brodie's waist. "This is Gabrielle, my wife. This is Ash and Melody...I'm sorry, I didn't catch your last names."

"Melody Silvers. And..." Mel quickly glanced around the room. "...Asher Pilsner."

Gabrielle smiled. "Nice to meet you."

"We're done here. Why don't you follow me back. I'll get you settled in and get you the key."

"Sounds good."

Mel finished her ginger ale and we walked to the truck.

"Pilsner?" I said to Mel as we got in the truck to follow Brodie to the cottage.

"It was the only name I could think of. And, I thought you didn't want them to know who you were yet. I saw the name on the wall and went with it."

"It's a beer."

"Technically, it's a pale lager, according to the sign at the bar."

I shook my head and laughed. "You're crazy."

She shrugged. "Maybe. But this is sort of fun, don't you think?"

"You could have used my middle name. Becket."

"I could have, but you said you didn't want them to know who you were yet, and you never know, that last name might sound familiar if your dad ever mentioned your mom to them.

I doubted he had, but she was right. "You sure you're going to be okay with this sleeping arrangement?"

"I guess. We'll think of something, but I didn't want to make them suspicious about who we were. It seemed more likely that a couple would be traveling together rather than just a guy and his friend who was a girl."

"What would be strange about that?" I asked, not quite understanding why that would be so hard to accept.

"I don't know, Asher. You didn't give me any instructions before we got here. I'm just going with my gut, and it just felt better to say we were a couple rather than just friends."

We pulled into a gravel driveway that seemed to go on forever. Red and pink carpet roses flanked each side. We stopped in front of a two-story farmhouse that sat on what looked to me like an acre of grassy land leading into a forest area in the back. The house had a wooden porch wrapping around the entire front, complete with a two-seater swing and a couple of comfortable looking chairs. A tiny pang of jealousy crept up my spine. Did they grow up here in this house?

We got out of the truck and Gabrielle waited with us while Brodie headed in to get the key. The sound of crunching tires came from behind us as another car pulled up behind my truck. Jackson and Lena stepped out.

"Could I use your bathroom?" Mel asked.

"Sure, come on," Gabrielle led her inside.

"I'm coming, too," Lena said. "I want to see what you did with the spare bedroom you just redecorated."

"Our place is just down the road," Jackson said, pointing to his left. "This old farmhouse belonged to my uncle. He left it to Brodie when he died. We used to live down the road that way." He pointed in the opposite direction of where he'd said he and Lena lived. We spent a lot of time in this house when we were kids. My mom, too, since my uncle was her only living relative and our dad died when we were young. Where did you say you were from?"

"I didn't, but San Francisco. Mel and I both grew up in the Bay Area. Now we live in the city. We perform at one of the local bars."

"Really? What do you perform?"

"We both play guitar and sing. I was doing it on my own up until last night. I invited Mel to play with me. It was something I'd been wanting to do for a while, and then when her brother died suddenly, well, it was time."

"That's too bad about her brother. Was it recently?"

"Yeah, a few weeks ago."

He nodded. "Well, it's great that you play. We'll have to jam sometime."

"Sounds fun."

He nodded. "What's up in Oregon, if you don't mind me asking?"

"No. It's fine. We're heading up for a vacation. Since Mel's brother just died and my mom passed away a couple of weeks before that, we just needed to get away for a while. Clear our heads."

"Sorry to hear that. Is your dad still alive?"

"No. He's been gone a long time now."

Jackson nodded. "I know what that's like."

I bet he did. I suddenly had this desire to come clean and tell him who I really was, but right then, Brodie and all the women came back out.

"Great chatting with you, Ash. I'm serious about getting together to jam. Come by the bar tomorrow night. We start playing at eight." Jackson and Lena got in their SUV and headed out. Mel and I followed Brodie around to the back and up the stairs to the cottage above the garage. It was small, but it did have a kitchen. It even had one of those stackable washer and dryers installed inside a closet.

"This is the bed," Brodie said as he yanked on a handle in the wall and a fully-made bed with sheets and a comforter flowed out. "The pillows are in the closet by the bathroom. The bed doesn't close all the way when you leave them in."

"Looks comfy."

"It's not too bad. There are clean towels in the bathroom, and in the kitchen you'll find some staples such as salt and pepper and other condiments. I suggest taking inventory before you go out for groceries if that's what you want to do. There are plenty of pots and pans for cooking, just make yourselves at home. I only ask that you put all dirty dishes and pots in the dishwasher, add a little soap— it's under the sink—and hit the start button when you decide you want to check out."

"Thanks. We'll be sure to take care of everything. I appreciate your hospitality."

"No problem. I'm glad the place was vacant for you. The same goes for me about jamming with us. I overheard the end of your conversation with Jackson. I'm always up for that."

Brodie and Gabrielle left shortly after they clued us in on everything we needed to know about the small cottage— if you could call it a cottage. I closed the door to our new temporary living quarters. A one-room studio apartment with just one queen bed, in the wall. This was going to be interesting.

I hadn't been able to get Mel out of my head ever since we had sex three weeks ago. She grew more beautiful every day. Even when she'd been crying and moping around like it was the end of the world. Losing a brother was hard. Now I had two, right here in the same town, and I didn't even know how to tell them we were related. That was all just too much for one person's mind to handle. I plopped down on the bed that Brodie had left open then stretched out and closed my eyes.

I opened them when I heard some noise coming from the bathroom. The sound of drawers opening and closing, then water running. I got up and cracked open the door. "Mel?"

She turned around to look at me, toothbrush in her mouth and her shirt partially unbuttoned. She pulled the brush out from between her lips and gave me a foamy white smile. "Sorry if I woke you."

"I wasn't sleeping. Just relaxing. You okay?"

She spit out the toothpaste in the sink. "Yeah. I wanted to clean up a little after being sick earlier, brush my teeth and wash my face. That's all. I felt like yuck, you know?"

I nodded. "Is your stomach better?"

"Yeah, actually. I feel great. The carsickness, or whatever it was, must have gone away. After I clean up, maybe we could grab something to eat somewhere."

"Sounds good."

I started to close the door. "Asher?" My name was barely a whisper on her lips. It was soft and sounded like she'd said it because she wanted me. I mean *really* wanted me, like in the shower with her a few weeks ago.

"Yeah?"

"I'm glad you decided to come here. I think your brothers are nice guys."

"Yeah, I know. Me, too."

She sucked in her lips and toyed with the last button on her shirt. My cock hardened inside my pants. There was no way I could continue this way.

Chapter Twenty

Melody

Here we were, alone in this small room with only one bed. This had to be a test. If this were a test, I had a feeling we were going to fail. Or succeed, whichever way you looked at things. Asher's eyes followed my finger as I circled it around the last button on my blouse. As they traveled back up to my face, he stepped closer, just one step inside the door. The way he stared at me made my stomach flip a little. Not like before when I'd been sick, this was a good feeling. The tender area between my thighs throbbed and became damp as I remembered how his lips had felt on mine. How his fingers had played between my thighs when I had showered with him.

Seeing him look at me the way he was had me wanting to be in his arms. So badly. I wanted to ask him to hold me. Just as I had that thought, he closed the distance between us and palmed my cheeks with his hands as his lips found mine. My arms went around his waist and my hands slid up his back. He kissed me slowly, and his fingers tangled in my hair. I moaned into his mouth, and he moaned with me. His lips brushed down my neck and my legs became weak, but his strong arms held me up.

"What are you doing?" I breathed against his chin.

"Do you want me to stop?"

"I thought…"

"Shhhh. You think too much sometimes, Mel."

I rested my head against his chest as he kissed the nape of my neck. I didn't want him to stop.

"I can hear your heart beating."

"That's a good thing. Always a plus."

"I agree."

"Do you know why I wanted you to come with me?"

"Because I'm your best friend and you needed me."

"Yeah. That's true. I do need you. But the reason I wanted you to come with me is because I can't stop thinking about you and I don't want you to be with anyone else while I'm gone. Not anyone, especially not Alex."

"Asher, when I went out with Alex, I…we…"

"Don't," he said and kissed me again. Softly, gently. I wanted to tell him that Alex and I never had sex. That he'd been right about him all along, but his kisses kept my tongue too busy and I soon forgot all about Alex. All I could think about now was Asher and his hands as they roamed down my thighs, finding their way between them and fingering me outside of my jeans. My panties were going to be soaked.

As our lips pressed together and our tongues mingled— sweet Jesus!—his hand was on my butt and he pulled me tight against him. His hard erection pressed into my thigh and his hand slipped just inside the waistband of my jeans.

"Asher, we shouldn't." I had no idea why I'd said that because, at that moment, I knew I wanted him more than I wanted to breathe.

"Why not?"

"Because…I…we—" The words lodged in my throat as he licked and kissed a sensitive spot on my neck right below my ear. My toes tingled. "I don't want to ruin us."

"Are we ruined?"

"No, but…"

"Then we won't be."

"But what happens when we get home?"

"I don't know. If you don't want me to go any further, tell me no, Melody. Otherwise, shut up and kiss me."

I kissed him.

As we kissed, our tongues did a frantic and desperate tangling as he unbuttoned my jeans and slipped the zipper down, then reached his hand down my pants and moaned. "Oh, baby, you are so wet for me."

We stopped kissing and I inhaled deeply as though I hadn't been able to breathe. He pulled his hand out of my pants as his fingers dipped under my shirt then pulled it up over my head, not even trying to deal with the rest of the buttons.

He took a step back, and I watched his eyes roam from my face to my breasts as he slowly ran his tongue over his lips. Oh so sexy.

"I need you, Mel. There hasn't been anyone else since you. I can't even look at another woman without thinking about you."

I opened my mouth, again, to tell him about Alex, but he smothered my lips with his while he shoved my pants to the floor. I stepped out of them. I was super glad to know he hadn't been with Lisa, but I decided to put off telling him about Alex. I had a feeling that just the mention of Alex's name would ruin this moment.

He stepped back again, and once again his eyes roamed down my body. He smiled and pulled his t-shirt over his head. I loved looking at his chest. Just the sight of him had me hot and wanting. He unbuttoned his jeans and I watched with a great amount of anticipation as the zipper went down. His pants and boxers hit the floor, and he kicked them away. His thick cock jutted forward, long and hard. He stepped to me again and kissed me before he tugged me over to the bed and sank back, pulling me on top of him, our lips never parting. My legs were spread over his hips, and he gyrated under me, pressing his cock against my clit as he sucked my nipples, teasing with his fingers and massaging his palms over them, sending strong thumping pulses into my lady parts.

When he dipped two of his fingers inside me and circled his thumb around my nub, I moaned and bucked my hips forward, feeling a surge of the slick wetness he was creating.

"You like that, don't you, Mel?" His words were heated and heavy with lust. So sexy.

He placed his hands on my hips and gently urged me up onto my knees as he rubbed his cock over my entrance. When he tugged me back down, I felt the stretch of my walls as he entered, and Asher groaned something like, "Fuck, you feel so good," as I slid down. His balls tickled my backside as he moved my hips. Even though we'd done it a few times that night weeks ago, I was still expecting the initial shock and pinch that I'd had the first time, but it never happened. His hands were strong, and he used his strength to thrust me up and then back down again, keeping rhythm with his own thrusts. When I lifted up, I looked at Ash and he was watching me, his eyes heavy-lidded and barely open. When I slipped back down on him, he grabbed my waist with both of his hands and with one swift motion, he pivoted my body onto my back and then positioned himself on top of me without losing connection. When his thrusts became stronger and harder, it was as if heaven opened up with roars of thunder in my head. I was floating on clouds as the intensity of the pressure built up inside of me.

This time was so much different than the last time. It wasn't as calculated and smooth as before. This time, it was heated and full of passion. As though Asher really wanted me and wasn't just doing everything so that I had a great experience. This time, we weren't just fucking—as Asher had put it—this time, we were making love, and the look in his eyes told me that he wanted me. I screamed as Asher shoved into me and we climaxed together. As his mouth took mine, our tongues collided, still urgent for one another and full of passion.

He sank down beside me and tugged me in close. Our breaths still panting. I closed my eyes. I didn't think I could be any happier than I was right at that moment.

When our breathing returned to normal, Asher whispered into my ear. "That, Melody, was not fucking."

"What was it?" I asked.

"It was making love."

I smiled. Was every dream I'd ever had, every fantasy I'd ever had about Asher Beaumont actually beginning to come true?

"Mel, I don't know what's going to happen when we go home, or what the future holds for us. But right now, I want you to know that I want you in my life. Not only as my best friend, but also as my lover."

I wasn't sure exactly how to interpret that, but I didn't want to screw this up by asking for more than he was willing to give me, so I stayed silent and let him kiss me with a tenderness that I hadn't felt from him before.

Asher turned on to his side and tucked me in close so my rear pressed against his groin. His arm draped over my shoulders and his fingers tangled with mine.

"So, how do you think I should break the news to Jackson and Brodie?" Asher asked in a low, soft voice.

"I think the best way is to just say it."

"Yeah, that's the hard part."

"But you need to have both of them present when you do."

"Maybe tonight. They invited us to jam with them at the bar."

"Do you think a public place like that is best? I mean, in a room full of people it might be hard to have a conversation about it. And I'm sure they are going to have a ton of questions."

"You might be right. Let's get dressed. I'm starving. You?"

I was hungry. I'd lost everything I'd eaten earlier after the long car ride through some winding roads. "Yeah. A cheeseburger sounds great."

"My thoughts exactly."

Chapter Twenty-One

Asher

We found a small café in town. Small was an understatement. It only had four, square, wooden tables inside. I went to the counter to buy the food while Mel sat at the only available table. I ordered a cheeseburger smothered with grilled onions, mushrooms, and a side mountain of French fries at her request, and a turkey club and a Caesar salad for me. She only ate half of her burger and a just few of the fries. I ended up eating the other half as well as the rest of her fries. I sort of knew that would happen.

I was feeling anxious about talking to Brodie and Jackson and wanted to get it over with. I should have just told them who I was when we'd first met, but it hadn't seemed like the best time.

By the time we finished eating, it was dark. We drove back to the bar to see if Brodie and Jackson were there. Playing some tunes might be a great way to break the ice.

We could hear music as we opened the truck doors. Mel and I grabbed our guitars from the back seat and went inside. Jackson waved us over the minute he saw us. He seemed excited about playing with us. It was a good feeling.

"What kind of guitar do you have?" Brodie asked as I pulled it out of the case

"D-28 Dreadnought."

"Jack's got a Dreadnought. Are you as picky about who touches yours as he is?"

"Probably." I chuckled. "What do you have?"

"I own a Fender Squier P Bass."

"That's right. You're the bass."

"Somebody's gotta do it."

I was nervous at first and missed a few beats, which pissed me off. I never screwed up like that. Even Mel gasped and commented on it.

"Asher! What the hell?"

I shrugged. Then Jackson skipped a few noticeable chords, but he only looked up and smiled. I suddenly didn't feel so awkward. We played several tunes together. Everyone falling right into the groove without another missed beat, none that I noticed anyway.

"You two been playing together long?" Brodie asked me.

"No, well, we've messed around some, but just really started playing together this past week." I had to grin as I glanced up to see Mel's smile. I knew she'd caught on to the "messed around" innuendo.

"Well, it sounds like music is in your blood."

"No doubt," I said.

It had been an awesome experience playing songs with my brothers. But the secret looming over our visit needled my brain constantly. I had to figure out a way to tell them who I was. Once again, I thought that I should have told them when I'd first met them. Now it might be too late, and they might get pissed that I'd waited.

The next couple of days flew by. Every minute had been packed full and there was never a dull moment. We jammed with Jackson and Brodie each night, and Mel and I made love every time we were alone. But I still hadn't gotten the nerve to confess the real reason why Mel and I were there to the guys. I was enjoying the time with her, and though I knew I had to tell them, I didn't want to spoil the special and new time Mel and I were spending together, getting to know each other more as lovers rather than just friends.

By the third day, Mel and I had just had our tenth orgasm together—by Mel's count. She was the one keeping score and it made me laugh. She stood in the shower. I stepped in and began sudsing down her front.

"Let's just knock on the door and see what happens," Mel suggested. "The sooner you tell them, the sooner you'll be able to relax and stop worrying about it."

"I know, you're right. It's just difficult."

"What's so hard? 'Hey, Jackson and Brodie, guess what? I'm your brother?'"

I laughed. "Yeah. That should work."

"In my experience with difficult situations, it's best to be as direct as possible."

"In *your* experience? What experience have you ever had with telling two people that you were related?"

"Well, none, but if I had two *more* brothers…" She lowered her eyes and I felt horrible for what she must be feeling. Here we were, talking about the fact that I had two brothers and couldn't find the courage to tell them who I was, when her own brother, whom she'd probably give anything to talk to one more time, had just died. But then she surprised me when she finished with, "…you can bet your pretty, twenty-inch cock that I wouldn't be hemming and hawing about letting them know about me."

I cracked up. "Twenty-inches? You always were horrible at math."

She giggled.

We finished our shower and dressed then headed down the stairs of the cottage. I took her hand as we walked up the four short steps to the front door of the main house. I pulled up the large brass knocker and let it bang down against the door three times, not too hard, but not too soft. Three times seemed like the norm. Wasn't that how many times people usually knocked on a door? My mind was rambling out of control with unnecessary trivial crap. When the door opened, I took a step back.

"Hey, Ash." Brodie looked at Mel and smiled. "Is everything all right upstairs?"

"Yeah. Fine. Listen." I paused and looked down at my grey Chuck Taylors as if they had the words I wanted to say etched into them. Mel nudged me in the side with her elbow when I didn't speak. "Can we talk?"

"Sure, come on in. Is everything okay?"

"Yeah, everything is great. Do you think you could call your brother and ask him to come over?"

He gave me a puzzled look. "Now you're starting to worry me."

"I swear nothing is wrong. I just wanted to talk to you both about something and it would be best if he was here, too." Mel squeezed my hand as if she tried to transfer all her positive energy to me. It made me feel good.

"Have a seat," he said, pointing to the sofa. Mel and I sat side by side on it, and Brodie sat on the piano stool staring at us as he pulled his cell phone out of his pocket and pushed a couple of buttons then held the phone to his ear and waited a couple of seconds before speaking into it. "What are you doing…? Good…come on over…yeah…yeah…I don't know…Ash and Mel are here and want to talk…I don't know…yeah…okay." He pushed a button on his phone and looked at us. "He'll be here in a couple of minutes."

Gabrielle walked into the room. "Oh, hey." Her smile was large and welcoming.

"Beer?" Brodie asked.

"Sure, thanks." A beer was probably a great idea. Something to knock the nerves down a notch.

"How about you, Melody?" Gabrielle asked.

"Okay. That would be nice, thank you."

"Sierra Nevada or Corona light?"

"Corona is fine," I said, knowing Mel didn't like many beers, but I knew she liked Corona and I didn't want to complicate things.

A minute later, Gabrielle came out with four bottles of Corona, a wedge of lime sticking out of the top of each one.

The front door opened, and Jackson and Lena walked in with Rufus at their heels. The dog immediately came over to Mel and me and we patted him on the head before he took off and made himself comfortable over by Jackson. "Hey, so, what's going on?" he asked then sat in a chair to the side of the sofa as Lena sat on the arm of it next to him. Gabrielle planted herself on the other side of Mel toward the end of the couch.

"Is something wrong?" Jackson asked Brodie.

"Don't know. Ash said he wanted to talk to us, together. That's all I know," Brodie said.

I took a sip of the beer and looked up at Brodie then at Jackson. I'm sure my face was pale from fear, nervousness, anxiety. I had no idea how they were going to receive this news I was about to lay on them, but we shared a father, and they had a right to know. I decided to just say it. "I…uh…my father's name was Charles Rutherford Beaumont," I said then took another sip of my beer.

"What?" Brodie said.

"Wait, what did you just say?" Jackson asked.

"My father's name was Charles Rutherford Beaumont. My last name is Beaumont. My mother gave me my father's last name even though they were never married."

"You're shittin' me," Brodie said. "How…I mean, you just walk in here out of the blue and tell us this and expect us to believe you?" Brodie stood up, and I edged back, unsure of what he was going to do. I thought maybe punch me or something.

"Wait," Jackson said.

"What, you believe him?" Brodie glared at Jackson and then back at me. Mel wrapped her fingers around mine.

"There's no reason for him to make something like this up, Brodie. What would be the point? It's not as if there's any money, some big family fortune to inherit. Dad died years ago, and he'd left us long before that, we knew he was seeing someone. Mom knew."

"Which brings me to the question, why now? Why did you wait until just now to come here?" Brodie asked. "And how old are you?"

"Brodie," Gabrielle placed her hand on Brodie's arm. "Sit down. Give him a chance to explain."

Brodie glanced at her, and I was thankful that he listened to her and sat down. This was hard enough without worrying about whether or not he was going to get violent.

"I'm twenty-one."

"Now, see? That…that's just proof that this is crazy. You're twenty-one and I'm twenty-three, and you expect us to believe that our father got your mother pregnant while he was still living with our mother. When I was just one and a half years old? That he cheated on our mother all those years?"

"I'm sorry," I said, but I wasn't really and decided to show my true colors. I wasn't a wimpy, snot-nosed little brother. I was a grown man and I had balls. I needed to stick up for myself, my mom. I wasn't afraid of these two guys. "No, actually, I take that back. I'm not sorry. I'm here. I was born. I'll admit not into the most perfect world and situation, but my mother…" I swallowed at the mention of my mom. "…she loved him. Yeah, he was an asshole and got her pregnant while he was still married to your mother. And he only came around to act like a father to me a couple of times in my life, so, yeah, big asshole. I never wanted to meet you. In fact, I spent my entire life hating you. Hating the life, the family that you had and I didn't. Hate is actually too nice of a word. I despised you. And him." I pointed to Jackson. "Look, this is stupid." I stood up, grabbed Mel's hand and pulled her up with me. "I can tell this was a mistake. We'll go upstairs and collect our stuff and leave. Thanks for the beers and the room." I was glad Mel hadn't tried to resist my attempt to leave and insist we stick it out. It was clear to me that these guys weren't open to anything I had to say.

"Wait," Jackson said. "Don't go yet. I apologize for my brother."

"Don't apologize for me, Jack, this guy's nuts."

"You don't know that," Jackson defended me. "Brodie, you're being an ass. Before you start throwing out insults, let's hear him out."

"No. He's nothing but a lying sack of shit."

"Sit the fuck down, Brodie, and let's listen to what he has to say," Jackson yelled, and to my surprise, Brodie sank back down onto the stool next to Gabrielle. She placed her hand on top of his and that seemed to calm him, but not by much. He was a stick of dynamite ready to explode.

"Please, sit down, Ash. Is Ash short for something?" Jackson asked.

"Asher," I said and sat.

"Okay, Asher, we're listening. Please continue."

I cleared my throat and ran my hand through my hair, carefully choosing my next words. "As I said, I never wanted to come here. The only reason I'm here is because my mom asked me to come. She left me a letter that I didn't find until after she died. She convinced me that the two of you are as innocent in this as I am and that I shouldn't punish you or myself for what our father did. She told me that you, most likely, didn't even know that I existed, and I guess she was right about that. Anyway, I just thought you had a right to know."

"And you said your mother just recently died?" Jackson asked, remembering our first conversation.

"Yeah, three weeks ago. I found the letter among some important papers she left for me."

"I'm sorry. How did she die?" Brodie asked, surprising the hell out of me that he even spoke, let alone asked in such a calm and caring way. I gave him a quick glance, wanting to see his facial expression. It was somber.

"Cancer. She had a brain tumor. It took her within three months from the time the doctors found it."

"Sorry, that must have been hard," Jackson said.

I nodded. "I've known about you my entire life. My dad, our dad, used to brag about you." I cleared my throat and continued. "When I was four, he told me I had two big brothers and said how much they'd love to meet me. At the time, I begged to go with him when he left that day so I could meet you. He promised that someday I would, but we all know that never happened. The man was full of empty promises. That was the last time I ever saw him actually. He sent monthly checks, a little to help out, but they stopped when I was seven. Later, we found out through sources that he'd been killed in a car accident."

Brodie sighed and shook his head. Gabrielle wrapped her arm around him and tugged him a little. Jackson had his hand on Lena's thigh and they looked at each other with sorrow on their faces.

"I didn't come here for a pity party or to bring up bad shit," I said. "I don't want anything from you. I just wanted to meet you. Now that I have, we'll go." As I stood, I grabbed Mel's hand and motioned for her to stand.

We headed toward the door, but Mel placed her hand to her mouth again. "I'm sorry, could I use your bathroom?"

Lena nodded and stood, wrapping her arm around Mel's shoulder to lead the way. "Are you okay?" she asked and glanced back at Gabrielle, who was now on her feet following them.

Jackson, Brodie and I waited silently, listening to the sound of Mel vomiting. Again.

Chapter Twenty-Two

Melody

Lena and Gabrielle stood just outside the bathroom door. I could hear them talking, but I couldn't make out anything they were saying. I rinsed out my mouth and washed my face and hands then stared at the pale, pasty face in the mirror. Damn flu. God, I hated being sick. This would make leaving now really difficult. I didn't want to sit in the truck for three or four hours. I felt bad for Ash. Brodie hadn't been very receptive at all. Well, he had softened up a bit after Ash mentioned his mom dying, so I guess the guy wasn't a total ass.

I flinched at the faint knock on the door.

I wasn't sure I was ready to leave the bathroom just yet. I opened it slightly to see Lena and Gabrielle standing there.

"Um…can we come in?" Lena asked.

I opened the door the rest of the way, and they came in. Lena had an oblong shaped box in her hand. "We think you should use this." I glanced at the box again. It was a pregnancy test. My heart skipped a beat.

I shook my head. "I can't be pregnant. I'm on the pill," I said defiantly.

"Well, sometimes things just happen. Pills get skipped or taken late. It can happen," Gabrielle said.

"No. It can't. Not to me, Gabrielle."

"Just call me Gabby."

"Okay."

"Have you skipped any periods?"

"Um…it's hard to tell since I don't have regular periods. That's why I was on the pill in the first place. But I can't be pregnant. I've only just started having sex…" I thought about all the times over the past couple of days. We had done it about a month ago, but only once, well, three times that night. But I'd been sick on our way up here. "The first time was about four weeks ago. But I would know, right? I'd feel something."

"That could be what this is all about," Lena said, gesturing toward the toilet and I knew she meant the vomiting. "Are your breasts tender?"

I gave her a blank look and nodded. Remembering that I'd read that somewhere, but I thought mine were tender just from being touched so much recently, or from PMS. I searched my memory, thinking about the pills. Then it dawned on me. That night with Asher, I'd been so excited about doing it with him. And then after feeling so good and euphoric, I'd completely forgotten. Shit, shit, shit. I did skip one. Damnit, and it had been right after Ash and I had sex. Oh no!

"Oh, crap…I may have skipped a pill," I said. "Can it happen that easily?" I had no clue about these things. I'd never had to worry about them before. I hadn't considered that this would happen. I'd always thought I was safe with taking the pill. The nurse had told me that if I skipped one to just take it as soon as I remembered. But she didn't mention not to have intercourse with anyone right around that time.

"Yeah, it can," Lena said. "Here. Just stick this end under the stream of pee and then call us when you finish."

They left me alone. I did need to pee, so that was lucky. If there was *anything* lucky about any of this. Maybe lucky was the wrong word. I pulled my jeans down and sat on the toilet, holding the stick under me as I tinkled on it. God, I wanted to cry.

After I had finished, I placed the stick on the counter and pulled up my pants. I opened the door and let the two women back in. I was grateful they were there, actually. I'd never had girlfriends, except for Erica. It was nice that they seemed so concerned for me and were willing to stand by me while I waited the three excruciatingly long minutes to see a plus or minus sign. I said a quick prayer for the negative one.

Lena stared at her cell phone's timer. I watched the stick. When the little window showed a plus sign, my knees wobbled and I sank down on the closed toilet seat and cried. This was not supposed to happen.

Gabby put her hand on my shoulder. "It will be okay. First thing you need to do is tell Ash."

I looked up at her and shook my head. "No. I can't. I…I told him I was on the pill. He trusted me. I can't tell him."

"You need to tell him. He would want to know. Once you tell him, then we'll all be able to figure out what to do," Lena said.

I look at her through blurry tears. "All?"

"You're family," she said.

"But, you all just now found out that Asher is Brodie and Jackson's brother."

"I know my husband," Lena said. "There is no way in hell he is going to let you and Asher just walk away now that he knows. Believe me, it's not in his DNA." She laughed.

"And Brodie is coming around. He's not the big oaf he sometimes appears to be," Gabby added. "You can trust us, Melody. We're practically sisters."

"But Asher and I aren't married or anything." I honestly didn't know what we were anymore. Best friends, boyfriend and girlfriend, lovers, fuck buddies? What were we? I looked at my hands holding the stick with the looming plus sign. "Hell, we were only just best friends up until this week."

"What do you mean?"

"Ash and I have known each other our whole lives. We've been best friends since we were about three or four. He and I...well, he was helping me." They looked at me like I was nuts.

"Helping you do what?" Gabby asked with a frown.

"Lose my virginity."

"What?" Lena asked.

"I mean, I wanted to have sex. I was going to do it with this guy. Anyway, Asher can't stand him and he didn't want me to do it with him, so he volunteered to be my first." This all sounded so stupid and immature as I laid the story out for them. But they didn't laugh at me or tell me how dumb and irresponsible I'd been. They simply listened to me.

Then there was a knock on the door. "Mel? What's going on?" It was Asher. "Can I come in?"

I dried my eyes then snatched the testing stick off the counter and held it behind my back. I opened the door. Asher stood with his arm on the door jam, and Jackson and Brodie stood down the hall a short distance away. Their handsome, frowning faces all very similar. The resemblance between them was uncanny. Lena and Gabrielle walked out ahead of me, ducking under Ash's arm. He seemed rather statuesque, and it was hard to figure out if he was mad or just concerned. I stuck the stick in my back pocket, not wanting him to see it.

I kept my back from him as we all headed to the other room.

"I don't think Melody is going to be able to travel today, Ash. It looks like you'll need to stay," Lena said with a small smile. Not quite happy, yet not upset. I hoped that meant that she wasn't happy for my situation, but I had the feeling that she wasn't upset that we had to stay either.

"What's wrong?" Asher asked.

"It's okay to stay," Jackson said. "I think I can speak for both Brodie and myself and say we'd like you to stay. I mean that. For a few days, let's get this all sorted out and see where it all leads."

We all looked at Brodie.

"Yeah, sure. I guess. Besides, if she's sick," Brodie pointed at me, "you can't really take off yet."

"I'll make some tea," Gabby said and took off for the kitchen.

"Let's all sit down. Maybe if we all get to know each other longer than a millisecond, we can figure out what to do. You have to understand, Ash, it's a shock for us. What you are telling us. Not something one expects to hear shortly after meeting someone," Jackson said.

"I get it," Asher said.

"Do you have a birth certificate?" Brodie asked Asher.

He nodded, opened his wallet, and pulled out a folded form. "I've been carrying it around ever since my mom died. The whole time I was contemplating coming here. I knew you would ask for it. I knew *I* would ask for one if someone came to me with this kind of news. I didn't want to forget to bring it with me so I stuck it in my wallet." He unfolded it slowly and handed it to Brodie.

Brodie took it and read it then passed it to Jackson. "This doesn't really prove that our father is your father. There are probably plenty of men named Charles Rutherford Beaumont."

Jackson gave his brother a quick glance. "What Brodie means is that—"

"I know what he means," Ash interrupted. "You want me to take a paternity test or something?"

"That would work," Brodie said.

"If you wouldn't mind," Jackson agreed. "Not that we don't believe you. I mean, I do. I believe that your father's name was Charles Rutherford Beaumont. But is that Charles Beaumont on your birth certificate the same Charles Beaumont that is our father? That is the question."

"He looks identical to the both of you," Lena said.

"That's true," Gabby agreed as she placed a tray on the small wooden coffee table. "Here, Mel, some saltine crackers. They should help calm your stomach some."

"Thanks," I smiled. The women in this family seemed a whole lot more accepting than the men.

Ash looked at me. "What's going on? Are you okay?"

I nodded.

Gabby cleared her throat and motioned to me with her eyes toward Ash. I knew what she was doing. She wanted me to tell him. Was I ready to? Now? In the middle of all this other chaos? I shook my head. She rolled her eyes at me, and I frowned. I wasn't ready to tell Asher, yet, not in the middle of everything else he had going on. It was just too much. I had to admit, though, it was nice that she was so concerned about me. Even if Ash were related to her husband, that didn't mean she had to instantly accept *me* into their family.

Chapter Twenty-Three

Asher

I understood where Brodie and Jackson were coming from. I didn't expect this to be walk-in-the-park easy. I'd probably be having the same questions if our father hadn't told me their names.

"I can agree to a paternity test if that would make you happy. But I know what the results will say. I don't think it's just some weird coincidence that my father would tell me I have two older brothers named Jackson and Brodie and that you were only a year or two older than me."

"You didn't say that before," Jackson said. "You never said he told you our names. That makes a world of difference."

Then I remembered the picture of my dad and me that I'd stuck in my wallet and reached into my back pocket to pull out the billfold. I fingered the photo and slipped it free.

"I also have this." I handed it to Jackson and he studied it, smiled at me, then handed it to Brodie.

"That is most definitely Dad," Jackson confirmed, and I felt the weight of an elephant slip from my shoulders.

"He talked about you a lot to my mom. He even told her you lived here in Turtle Lake. I'm sorry that he wasn't the man you always thought he was. But I'm not responsible for what he did, and neither are you."

Both Jackson's and Brodie's eyes shot to mine at the same time.

"You're right," Jackson said. "We aren't."

"I'd still like to see some kind of DNA test results. Plus, how the hell could your mother and our father have been so irresponsible to have a kid knowing he was already married and had small children?"

Sniffles commenced beside me as Mel started crying.

"Mel?" I said.

Gabrielle stood and held out her hand to Brodie. "Come on. Let's take a walk."

"What? Fuck no. I don't need a walk, I need some answers."

"Brodie. Come with me, please, I would like to talk to you. In private."

"Jesus Christ." He got up and followed her.

"How could you say that, Brodie? You of all people should know that you should be more considerate about mistakes when it comes to love," Gabrielle said as they left the room.

"Jackson, let's give them some privacy," Lena said, and she and Jackson got up.

"Privacy? Why do we need privacy? Mel?" I had trouble controlling the panic in my voice. What the hell was going on?

Melody sat there studying her hands as her fingers intertwined nervously in her lap. "I'm pregnant," she whispered.

"What?"

"I'm pregnant." She reached behind her and pulled out a white plastic stick that looked similar to a thermometer. I instantly knew what it was. She handed it to me. "It has a plus sign. That means I'm pregnant."

This fucking day was just not getting any easier. "I'll kill Alex," I said, barely audible and through very clenched teeth. But she heard me.

"What?"

I stood up and took a couple of steps away. "I said I'm going to kill that fucking asshole, Alex."

Her eyes grew wide and she started sobbing. "God, Mel, I'm sorry. I don't mean to be so crass. I'm sorry he did this to you. But you know I hate him, I have since high school. You're not the first one he's done this to, you know."

She stopped crying a stared at me.

"You remember. Shannon Bright? He got her pregnant in eleventh grade. She had to drop out of school. When Shannon told Alex that she was pregnant, he shrugged her off and accused her of sleeping with other guys. He laughed at her and told her tough fucking luck, he said it couldn't possibly be his. She was going to have an abortion. We were friends, and she begged me to go with her for support. I reluctantly agreed, but she changed her mind anyway, the day before when her mom found out. Her mom was actually cool about it after a few hours of tears, and agreed to help Shannon with the baby. But my point is, now he's done it again. To you. *My* best friend. I'm going to kill his sorry dick-faced ass."

Mel wiped her tears with the back of her hand and stood up. "Asher. You're an imbecile." And then she walked out of the house, leaving me standing in the living room by myself.

"What the fuck?"

Gabrielle came running inside. "What happened? What did you say to her?"

I watched as Brodie and Jackson came in. Lena must have stayed out with Mel. God, I should be with Mel, not a stranger.

"I need another beer," Brodie said and headed to the kitchen. "Anybody else want one?"

"So, you all know?" Gabrielle and Jackson nodded. "Of course, you know. You gave her the pregnancy test." I pointed at Gabby.

Gabby nodded. "I'm sorry, Ash. But what did you say to her that made her come running out crying?"

"I told her I was going to kill Alex."

"Who's Alex?" she asked.

My eyes shot to hers. "The guy that…" I slammed my stupid mouth shut when I saw the puzzled expression on her face. I ran my hand over my eyes to ward off the headache that threatened behind them. Mel hadn't mentioned Alex to them?

"Oh, fuck me. I am an imbecile."

"What do you mean?" she asked.

"Mel didn't sleep with Alex," I found myself mumbling aloud. "That's why she was home at eleven that night and not in Alex's bed. If she'd slept with him, she wouldn't have been home that early." I stopped my blabbering; realizing Gabby had no idea what the fuck I was talking about. Why hadn't Mel told me? Why did she let me go on thinking she'd been with him? Was I that much of an inconsiderate fool not to realize it? Apparently.

I left Gabby and Brodie in the house and found Mel sitting on the swing with Lena. She was still crying. I felt like a jerk. I slowly strolled over to them. Lena got up, placed her hand on my shoulder, and smiled at me then went inside.

I stood in front of Melody. "Mel, I'm sorry. I'm a jerk. "It's mine, isn't it?" *Please say it's mine,* I pleaded silently.

She nodded. My stomach tightened. Half with excitement and happiness, and half with fear.

"You were never with Alex, sexually I mean."

"No."

"When I told you that I hadn't been with anyone since you, why didn't you tell me then that you hadn't been with Alex?" I thought back to kissing her. Wishing I could kiss her right then and make everything better. Wishing I could hold her in my arms and take back all the references to Alex that I had made.

"Because you never gave me a chance, you started kissing me and…and then we were…you know, deep into it again. It slipped my mind."

"And after?"

"Alex was the last thing on my mind, and I didn't think it was necessary."

"Not necessary? How could you let me go on believing that you'd slept with Alex when you hadn't?"

She closed her eyes and inhaled a deep breath. "I didn't know you thought I had. Not really. And I didn't know I was pregnant, okay? I never thought I needed to tell you that I *hadn't* slept with someone because why even mention something that didn't happen and it really wasn't any of your business…until now. And anyway, I did try to tell you, but you kept kissing me and then…and then…I don't know,

Ash, my mind turns to oatmeal when you're kissing me and I didn't want to think about Alex."

I wanted to laugh at that but managed to stifle the smile. God, she was adorable. I simply nodded and sat down on the swing next to her, stunned silent.

Chapter Twenty-Four

Melody

When Asher accused Alex of getting me pregnant, my whole world collapsed. It was as if he'd completely discarded the fact that we'd had one, let alone several sexual encounters recently—the last that very afternoon.

He sat down on the swing beside me and I kept waiting for him to say something. But other than him asking me about why I hadn't told him about something that hadn't even happened, he hadn't uttered a word. In the house, he'd talked about some girl in high school that he'd been very willing to help, but when it came to his own mistake, he didn't seem capable of acknowledging it let alone helping me. It was all too much to bear. I guess, Shannon Bright had been lucky to have a mom so understanding. I doubted mine would be so accepting of something like this. First, she loses her only son in a horrific car accident, and then her only daughter disgraces her by getting pregnant. By the guy who doesn't want anything to do with her.

I couldn't take it anymore. I got up and headed down the steps. I didn't want to look at Asher. I could tell by the way he was acting that he didn't want me or the baby. God, what was I going to do?

I headed up the stairs to the cottage we were renting. I unlocked the door and walked inside. The bed was still down and the covers still bunched up in the middle. As much as I wanted to burrow myself into them and cry—possibly sleep—for about five hours and forget about the world, I couldn't. I couldn't bring myself to get on the bed—the bed that Ash and I had just made love on less than three hours ago—and snuggle into those sheets and covers that I knew would smell like him.

I opened my suitcase that sat on top of the wooden luggage rack. I pulled out my yoga pants. I wanted to get out of my jeans. Not that they were too tight, yet, I wasn't that far along. But they were a bit uncomfortable considering my stomach was at war with everything I put into it. If this were an indication of what type of child I was carrying, I was really in for a world of trouble. A single mom with a warrior to raise. Great. Just what I always wanted. Though, it was Asher's warrior, and even though he didn't want me, the idea that I'd always have a part of him started to sink in.

I was so tired. Before changing into my yoga pants, I decided to take a bath and ran some water in the tub. Maybe a soak in some warm water would make me feel better. As I sank down into the steamy water, I instantly began to relax. Yes, this was exactly what I needed.

I half expected Asher to follow me upstairs, but I was glad he hadn't. I needed to be alone to collect my thoughts.

This was a lot to process. I was going to have a baby. I was twenty-one years old. I could do this. My mom had been twenty when she had Ted, and by the time she was twenty-two she'd had me. But she'd had one important thing I didn't have. A loving husband. Well, at the time anyway. My dad wasn't in our lives much these days. I wondered how he would take being a grandfather. Would he be accepting, or would he be ashamed of me and think I was irresponsible. I had been irresponsible. Forgetting to take my birth control pills had been very irresponsible. No wonder Ash was so upset. He'd had sex with me thinking everything would be fine. It was supposed to be a one-night thing. He'd wanted to be my first. Saying he was my best friend and had known me his whole life. That it should be him. I had even told him I was taking the pill to ease his mind, though he already knew I was on them. He knew everything about me. Why had he doubted me about Alex, though?

After soaking in the tub and donning my stretchy yoga pants and a t-shirt, I gave in to the lure of the bed and bundled myself up in the covers. A few minutes later, I heard the door open. I felt the dip of the mattress beside me as Asher's hand gently grazed my shoulder. I opened my eyes. "Go away," I said.

"Mel. Come on. We need to talk about this."

"No. I don't want to talk to you. Not now, I'm too tired. Please, Asher, just go away and let me sleep."

I turned over to face the other way and closed my eyes. The last thing I remembered after that was hearing the door close. The room fell silent with just my own frustrating thoughts and me to fill it.

Chapter Twenty-Five

Asher

I'd sat outside on the swing for about forty-five minutes, getting up the nerve to go up and talk to Mel. I'd been a complete ass. I didn't know how to fix that. I didn't think there was a way. How do you take back accusing the woman you've known your whole life of sleeping with someone she never slept with? Accusing him of being the father of *your* child.

After Mel had told me to leave the cottage, I closed the door and just sat at the top of the stairs. I didn't know where to go.

I didn't feel right going into Brodie's house. The three of us still needed to talk, but I wasn't ready to talk about brothers, not now when I had to deal with being a father.

"I've been there." I looked up to see Brodie standing a few steps below me. He took the last two steps up, sat beside me, and handed me a beer. I took it. Mostly because my throat was raw and my mouth was as dry as sandpaper.

"Thanks." I took a large swig.

"Sure." He drank some from the other bottle he held. "I know what you're going through," he said. "I was wrong before when I called your mother irresponsible. Brothers or not, you didn't deserve that. I'm sorry."

"It's okay," I said."

"No, it's not." He sighed. "I'd gotten a girl pregnant shortly after we graduated from high school. Talk about irresponsible. I was so irresponsible on so many levels. To make a long story short, it didn't turn out very well. She didn't tell me she was pregnant until after she'd had an abortion. She never gave me the opportunity to want to be a part of her and the baby's life."

I had the beer bottle up to my lips to drink but stopped. He'd caught me completely off guard with that one.

"Wow. That must have been tough."

"Yeah. It took a long time to get over. Even though my experience is very different than yours and Mel's, I thought it might help to know that I sort of know what it feels like. At least the irresponsible part." He laughed.

"Mel won't even talk to me after what I accused her of. How could I be so stupid and actually think it was someone else's? She'll never forgive me for that, and I wouldn't blame her."

"I don't know, Ash. I've seen the way she looks at you. That look doesn't happen unless there's something there."

"One can only hope."

"Listen, about this brother thing..."

"Don't worry about it. As soon as Mel is ready, we'll leave and get out of your life."

He shook his head. "It's always been just Jackson and me. I feel sort of cheated, you know?"

"What do you mean?"

"Our dad. He told you about us, but he never told us about you. You've known for practically your whole life that you had brothers. You knew someday you'd meet them and you've been preparing for it. Things you might say, or how we might meet, possibly even looking forward to it. Maybe not consciously, but you know you have. Us, at least me, I'd never considered the possibility of having another brother. So I've never had that opportunity to wonder about you. You were a kid when he told you. You must have ached to know us, especially back then."

He was right about all that. I'd cried myself to sleep many nights, wishing I could be with the two big brothers I didn't know, yet admired. Eventually, my admiration turned to anger. Anger that they had each other and I had no one. But I kept all of that to myself. Maybe someday I'd say it all out loud.

"You sort of had an advantage over us. Coming here, introducing yourself, meeting us without letting on who you were. You had an opportunity to assess us before telling us who you were."

"It wasn't that I didn't want to tell you. I wasn't sure how to."

"Doesn't matter. I would have done the same thing." He downed the rest of his beer. "The more I think about it, though, I guess you're at the disadvantage now."

"How so?"

"Well, now, you're waiting on our approval of you."

One thing he didn't know. I'd been waiting for that my entire life. But I nodded.

"Go snag your guitar and let's go down and play some tunes."

Brothers or not, playing music was what I did to calm my nerves, and this entire day called for some serious jamming. I stood and opened the door slowly, careful not to wake Mel. I wanted to talk to her so badly. I peeked at her, resting peacefully, her chest moving up and down in precise increments, each breath giving life to *my* child.

I grabbed my guitar and quietly left her sleeping.

Brodie was halfway down the steps when I came out. We strolled in to the living room. Jackson sat in the chair, strumming away, and Lena sat at the piano. They were playing an old Bob Dylan song, *Forever Young*. Jackson glanced up and smiled as he sang harmony with the ladies. Gabrielle, who'd been sitting with Lena at the piano, stood and walked over to Brodie. He kissed her before reaching for his bass guitar. I took a seat on the sofa where I'd been before and took my guitar out of its case. I fell in without missing a beat. It was as if we'd been playing music together our whole lives.

When we finished that song, Jackson strummed a few chords of the next song without saying what it was, but I recognized it right away and kept up with him. He motioned for me to take the lead and I sang the words to Eric Clapton's *Wonderful Tonight*. As I started the second verse, Mel opened the door and walked in. Our eyes met and we stayed focused on each other. I swear it had to have been fate for her to enter right at the moment I was singing her favorite song, but this time, I sang it right to her, because she was beautiful.

She stood, listening to me sing.

Chapter Twenty-Six

Melody

I hadn't been prepared for the emotions that overpowered my heart as I listened to Asher sing my favorite song. I knew he knew it was my favorite, and the way he stared at me had goosebumps flowing up and down my arms. I didn't want to be mad at him, but I couldn't just turn off my feelings like that. His accusations about Alex had really hurt. He might be gorgeous, sitting there singing and playing his guitar, but he needed to take responsibility for things. However, I wasn't about to beg for his help. I'd come to terms with my situation while I'd slept and I knew I'd be able to deal with it all on my own if I had to.

The next week flew by, and Asher was getting to know his brothers as they had come to terms with him. It was great the way Jackson and Brodie had accepted Asher as their brother. I was glad for him, though I missed my own brother so much, particularly now that I knew I was going to have a baby. Teddy would have made a great uncle. I smiled thinking about that and then the tears came. Would Ted be upset about this? I didn't think so. He'd hinted so many times that Ash and I should be together. But I'm sure he hadn't imagined it turning out this way.

Ash played in the band with the Beaumont brothers in the bar, and after Jackson had introduced Asher as their little brother, the entire town embraced Ash as one of them with no questions asked.

Asher finally had everything he'd ever wanted. His brothers' acceptance and what looked like the beginnings of a loving relationship with them.

Brodie and Jackson really were great, and I was happy for Asher.

Though, my own life was a mess. Ash and I hadn't come to terms with the situation we were in, and we were barely speaking. This pregnancy was like adding oil to a fire. My mind was already so messed up from Ted's death, adding an unwanted baby into it only made things worse. Correction, unwanted by one of us. I was scared as hell, but the more I got used to the idea, I wanted a child—Ash's child—more than anything. I had dreams about whether it was a boy or a girl. I didn't care either way, but I pictured a little Asher every time I thought about a baby boy.

Nothing in my life was turning out the way I'd imagined it would. I'd spent so many days growing up daydreaming about Ash, wishing we could have the relationship we'd promised each other when we were kids. I certainly hadn't planned on having his baby without him being a part of it. The way he'd acted hurt so badly, and I hated him for it. I just couldn't forgive him. Whenever he tried to talk to me, I either walked away or put my headphones in my ears. After about three days of that, he stopped trying. It made staying in the cottage difficult, and Brodie told Asher he was welcome to stay in the guest room they had in the main house. Ash took him up on it almost immediately. That only made me hate him more. He didn't even want to try anymore it appeared. So it was as if I was living in that one-room cottage over the garage of strangers by myself.

God, I couldn't wait until I could go home and be in my own apartment and not have to deal with Asher. I'd considered taking a bus home, but I didn't have the money, and there was no way I was asking Asher for it. I stayed up in the cottage most of the time. I only left it when Lena or Gabby came up and asked me to go for a walk or have some tea with them. They'd become my salvation. Always making sure I was okay and including me whenever they went somewhere or just inviting me down to visit with them. A lot of times, we went to Lena's house just so we wouldn't run into Asher. They knew I was avoiding him, though they'd told me several times that even though they understood why I wasn't talking to Asher, they thought I should at least hear him out. But I wasn't ready to yet.

I was ready to go home though. Don't get me wrong. I loved hanging with Lena and Gabby. In the short amount of time that I'd known them, they'd become as close as sisters. But...I woke up missing my mom. She was going to be so pissed at us. Yes, I included Asher in that too because I knew how much she considered Ash a part of our family. And she'd been Nora's best friend so Ash was like another son to her.

Even though I was mad as hell at Asher, I still wanted him to have the time to get to know Brodie and Jackson. It would have been unacceptable for me to just tell Asher I wanted to go home without giving him a chance to spend time with the two men he'd always wanted to accept him for who he was. And they had, with open arms.

I got out of bed and jumped in the shower. I wanted to go find Asher and see if he was ready to leave. If he wasn't, then I was ready to ask for the money to take the bus home. I'd had enough with being angry at him. I just wanted to be in my own apartment and get the dreaded conversation with my mom out of the way.

After my shower, I shrugged into my yoga pants and t-shirt, my go-to outfit on this trip. I was all about comfort these days. I headed down the stairs and sat on the swing, waiting for some sounds of life from inside. I didn't want to wake anyone too early. I glanced at my phone, it was ten o'clock. I decided it was plenty late enough to knock, and if Asher was the only one in there sleeping, then he deserved to be woken up.

I knocked, but no one answered. I tried the doorknob. It turned, and the door slowly opened. I peeked inside but didn't see or hear anyone. I stepped in and looked around. I heard a faint sound from the kitchen so I headed that way.

"Hey, Mel. Good morning," a smiling Gabby said.

"Good morning. Um...sorry, I knocked but no one answered and the door was unlocked."

"No worries. Me casa, you casa. Or whatever that saying is." She laughed. "You look pretty this morning."

"I do?"

"Yeah. Your cheeks are full of rosy color and your eyes are bright. Looks like pregnancy is doing its thing."

"What thing?"

"You know, pregnant women always looks so beautiful, glowing with radiance. Of course, that might have something to do with you standing right in the sun's rays, which are making your blonde locks very vibrant. But, nonetheless, you are stunning this morning." She laughed. "Tea? I have some herbal decaf that has a hint of peach. It's very smooth and really good."

"Thanks. That sounds delicious."

She pulled a mug down from the cupboard and stuck a tea bag in it. Then poured hot water from a kettle that had been on the stove into the cup. "Honey?" she said, holding up a little plastic bear container half-full of honey.

"Yes, please. Thanks."

"Here you go." She handed me the cup steaming with something that smelled heavenly. "Have a seat," she said and sat in one of the chairs.

"Thanks." I sat in the other chair across from her and sipped the tea. "Hmmm. That's delicious."

"It's my favorite."

"Have you seen Asher this morning?"

"Yes. He left with Brodie and Jackson."

"Oh. Will they be back soon? I thought we would be leaving today. I'm getting a little homesick to tell you the truth. Plus, as much as I am dreading it, I need to tell my mom about the baby."

"You have time. If your mother is anything like mine, God forbid, there's no point rushing that one."

"I don't really know how she'll take it. I know she'll be disappointed in us. She considers Ash part of the family. My brother and Ash—well, me too—were best friends since childhood. Ash's mother and mine were very close."

"You said *were*. Did you decide to end your friendship with Ash?" Gabby asked.

"No. I said *were* because my brother just died a few weeks ago."

"Oh, God. Mel, I'm so sorry. Forgive me. I didn't know."

"It's okay. How could you know? I'm not sure Ash mentioned it. I know I didn't. Ash and I haven't even talked much about Ted. Well, we haven't talked at all since we found out that I'm pregnant."

"Yes. I know."

"I bet you all think I'm being silly about it, but I've known Ash my whole life and I can't tell you how much it hurt that he thought this baby was someone else's."

"I know I've said this before, but maybe he *was* just shocked about it. You were shocked, right? In fact, you didn't want to believe it at first."

"Yeah, I was. But that's different."

"Maybe. But it's pretty clear to all of us how much Ash cares about you. I think he asks where you are every hour of the day."

"I know he cares about me." As a friend. My mind raced to the first time we'd had sex in the cottage upstairs, how vague Asher had been about where our relationship was headed or where it was at that moment. "I'm just having a difficult time forgiving him for the way he acted when I told him I was pregnant. I never imagined he would think it was Alex's and not his. That just hurts, that's all."

"Hey, ladies. What am I missing in here?" Lena's all too cheery voice sang out as she entered the kitchen. "Hmmm...there are two too many gloomy faces in here. What's going on?"

"We're just talking about Ash's lack of tact," I supplied.

"Ohhhhh. That again. Well, I have a super idea that might help change the mood."

"Anything would be an improvement," I said.

"Since you've been here, you really haven't had a chance to see much of Turtle Lake. I thought since the sun is out and the temperature is up in the high 60's, maybe we could go shopping or have a picnic down by the lake. We could even take Jackson's small fishing boat out if you want. If we hit it around dusk, there might be a cool sunset."

"I think I should wait and talk to Ash first. I thought we were going home today."

Lena shook her head. "That's not what I heard. In fact, the boys are planning another jam session at the bar tonight."

I sighed. Fuck. That was just like Asher lately. Never bothering to ask me what I would like. Just going ahead and making his own goddamn plans without even consulting me. I was fuming mad, I could feel the steam coming from my nostrils.

"Don't be mad, Mel. We don't want you to leave yet. Come on. Let's go shopping and forget about Asher."

I shook my head. As fun as shopping with them sounded, I just couldn't. "I can't. I don't have any money."

"You won't need money to window shop. Most of the stores are just little souvenir type stores anyway. It's a cute town. We'll do some window shopping, then stop in at the corner grocery store and get some cheese and stuff for a picnic."

"That sounds fun," Gabby said, "I haven't really looked in those stores since I've been here."

It did sound like fun.

"Okay." I guess there really wasn't much I could do about leaving anyway. Not if I couldn't even ask Asher for the money for the bus. I looked down at my yoga pants and t-shirt. "Do I need to change my clothes?"

"No. What you're wearing is perfect," Lena said. "I'm wearing the same thing."

We strolled down the sidewalk on Main Street looking in all the little shop windows. There weren't very many. Nothing like San Francisco. But the few that were there did have some interesting pieces and trinkets that were made locally.

Lena hadn't been joking when she mentioned the corner grocery store. It was literally on the corner and about as big as a liquor store in San Francisco. We picked up some cheese, crackers, and some salami, along with some lemonade and headed out toward the lake.

It was a short two-minute drive to the lake, and Lena pulled the SUV into an open, gravel-covered area nestled between a cluster of trees. Gabby grabbed the bag of groceries, Lena grabbed the blanket, and I followed behind. We headed into the forest, following a small trail that led to the lake and I was suddenly in awe of my surroundings. This place was beautiful. The water was so pristine and glassy smooth; as if the lake had never been touched by humans.

"Here, help me spread this out," Lena handed me a side of the blanket.

We each ate some food and talked about our lives. They told me about how they'd met Brodie and Jackson. Lena's story was particularly interesting and it broke my heart to listen as she recounted it all. She'd had a rough life growing up, and an even rougher time until she'd met Jackson. Gabby's tale of how she and Brodie became a couple was sort of funny, and even she couldn't help but laugh at how stupid she'd been when she'd first met him. I told them all about my brother and Ash, the way we were always a threesome. How my brother had died. I even told them the story about how Ash and I had decided to have sex that first time. How I wanted to lose my virginity, and Ash volunteering.

"What red-blooded man wouldn't want to volunteer for that job?" Lena laughed.

Now that I thought about it, it was funny, but I felt a bit abased at how naïve I'd been. I nibbled on a piece of cheese as my cheeks warmed with chagrin.

"Sorry, Mel. I don't mean to make light of what happened. You told Ash—a gorgeous man, by the way—that you wanted to lose your virginity, and you told him you were going to have sex with the one guy he hated most. Of course, he would volunteer."

"I know. But I've been so stupidly in love with Ash my whole life, for me it was the best option possible," I admitted. "When he told me he wanted to be my first, I thought I'd heard him wrong. I couldn't believe he was telling me that my fantasy was about to come true. And now, because of my stupidity and forgetting to take my pill, I'm going to have his baby. I didn't trick him into a baby, though. I want you to know that. I really did forget about the pill. I was so high on the experience of being with him that it didn't occur to me that missing a pill would be a problem. Then when my brother died, I forgot to take it a couple more times."

"We know you didn't trick him," Gabby said.

"Do you think he thinks that?"

"No. At least, he's never said that. No. I seriously doubt he thinks that," Lena said. "No one thinks that."

"I hope not."

"Hey, let's take Jackson's boat out. Do you know how to work it, Lena?

"I think so. It has a motor. What could be so hard?" We got up and headed toward what looked like a pile of brush. She shoved the branches away to reveal a small, metal boat that lay upside down. "Give me a hand." She placed her hands on the edge and Gabby and I flanked her on each side and lifted it up and over. It was a small boat with a small outboard motor.

"This looks fun," I said.

We pushed and shoved it into the water, getting our feet wet in the process. Then we all hopped in when the motor cleared the silt and the prop became completely submerged.

"I hope you know what you're doing," Gabby said.

"Don't worry. I've seen Jackson do this all the time."

"Wait, shouldn't we pick up the blanket and stuff first?" I asked, pointing back at the grassy area with our stuff.

"I'm sure it will be fine. We won't be out very long."

Once we were a safe distance from the shore, Lena pulled the cord on the motor. It started right up. The view was gorgeous. I'd never seen a lake so calm and smooth. Like glass. We traveled down the lake until I could barely make out the blanket we'd left on shore. As we headed farther into the lake, we turned a corner after passing some land that jutted out into the middle and then we headed into a wider part of the lake. "This lake is a lot larger than I thought." My eyes about popped out of their socket at the sight of snow-covered peaks. "Is that Mount Shasta?" I asked.

"Yeah. Isn't it gorgeous?" Lena answered, beaming with pride. "I love this lake. I love coming out here with a good book and just sitting here in the boat while Jackson fishes."

I dipped my fingers into the water. "Burr. This water is so cold. Does it freeze in the winter?"

"No. It's not cold enough since this lake sits right in the heart of a valley. We occasionally get some snow, but it melts pretty quickly."

We kept on going for about fifteen more minutes.

Gabby looked up at the sky and pointed. "It looks like some clouds are coming in. So much for our warm sunshine."

The clouds came in quickly, and along with them wind.

"We should probably head back. I don't like the look of those clouds," Lena said as the wind blew her long, red locks into her face. She swiped them away, but it was no use, they just kept coming back. The strong wind was blowing all our hair out of control.

Gabby reached into her pocket and came out with some hair bands. She handed one to me and one to Lena.

"Thanks," I said, taking the elastic and pulling my hair back into a ponytail. Lena did the same.

"I usually have a spare or two," Gabby said and started laughing.

"What's so funny?" I asked.

"The three of us would make a great Clairol commercial. A redhead, a blonde, and a brunette," she said while pointing at each one of us as she said the hair color.

The wind got stronger and I shivered. All I had on was a t-shirt and my yoga pants. I'd left my hoodie back on the blanket where we'd been picnicking. It had been sunny, and the warm rays had felt good on my arms. In fact, that was close to what we all had on, except Lena wore a pale blue button-down, long-sleeved blouse instead of a t-shirt. But it was thin, and I could tell she was just a chilly as I was.

As Lena turned the boat around, the engine sputtered and then stopped.

"What happened?" Gabby asked.

"I don't know. It just stopped." She stood up and pulled on the cord to start it again. It came right back on.

"Whew," I said, but I spoke too soon as the motor sputtered and stopped again.

"Dammit! What is wrong with this thing?" Lena whined and pulled on the cord once more; the engine cranked and whined but wouldn't turn over. She tried again, and again, and again. Still nothing. "My fingers are getting raw."

"Here, let me try," Gabby pulled it a few times, but still nothing."

"Wait. You're flooding the engine," I said. I didn't know too much about boats, but I knew if you cranked too long on the gas peddle trying to start a car, it would make things worse.

"What?" They both looked at me, their foreheads wrinkling with bewilderment.

"If you try to start it too many times, the engine will flood from too much gas," I explained then blew my warm breath on my fingers that were becoming numb from the cold. My arms were cold, my feet were cold too since my socks and Converse were still soaking wet. "Let it sit for a few minutes and then try it again."

They nodded and Gabby sat down.

"The wind is getting stronger by the minute," I said.

"It's going to get colder, too. The wind is blowing all the cold air from the mountain down this way."

"Are there any oars?"

"There should be one," Lena said, glancing around the small boat floor, but none of us saw one. "It must have fallen out when we flipped the boat over. I didn't notice it. Sorry." Lena sank down and sat in the floor of the boat. "Come down here, it helps a little."

Both Gabby and I moved to the floor. The sides of the metal boat weren't very high, but they did help block some of the wind.

After about ten minutes Gabby said, "Maybe we should try again?" She stood and pulled on the cord to start the motor, but this time, it didn't even try to catch. There was barely a sputter.

"Are we out of gas?" I asked.

"No. I checked it before we left. It was almost full. We haven't gone that far, there should be plenty of gas still." Lena got up and unscrewed the cap and peeked inside the tank. "Yep. There is plenty of gas."

"God, what are we going to do? The water is too cold to swim to shore. We're stuck out here in the middle of the lake. Did anyone bring their phone?" Gabby asked.

I shook my head, "I left it in my jacket. No pockets to carry it."

"Same here," Lena said. None of us had pockets, so all of our phones were back on the picnic blanket with the food and our jackets while we sat stranded in the middle of a freezing lake.

Great.

Gabby got up to try the motor again. "Someone give me a hand. Maybe if two of us pull it will catch."

I got up since I was the closest and put my hand over Gabby's.

"On three. Ready?"

I nodded.

"One, two, three." We yanked on the cord and Gabby's elbow hit me in the chest, sending me backwards. I lost my balance and fell into the lake. My ankle hit the side of the boat on the way in and I thought I would die from the pain, except the shock of the cold water made me completely numb within seconds.

"Oh my God. Mel!" I heard Lena shout as cold water enveloped my body. I came up sputtering, teeth chattering.

"Take my hand," Gabby said. I did, and Lena grabbed onto my arm, pulling me back into the boat.

"Co...co...co...cold," I chattered out the word and sank down to the bottom of the boat to get out of the wind.

"I am so sorry, Mel," Gabby cried. "Are you okay?"

I shook my head. Tears stung my eyes, but I doubted that they noticed since I was soaking wet. "My ankle hurts. It hit the side of the boat."

"I can't believe I shoved you in the lake. God, Mel, I'm so sorry," she said again, and I nodded. I knew she hadn't done it on purpose, but I was freezing nonetheless, and my ankle was throbbing.

"We have to get back. Mel will freeze to death if we can't get that motor running," Gabby said.

They both tried to start the engine again, but it was no use. With the force of the wind, we drifted farther away from where we'd started. The chance of anyone finding us was slim.

My head swirled and my stomach twisted into a knot. "Oh, no," I cried and leaned over the edge, losing all the cheese and salami I'd eaten earlier. This baby didn't seem to care much for the cold water any more than I did.

I sat there shivering. Lena sat beside me and wrapped her arms around me. "You'll get all wet," I said.

"That's okay. You need to keep warm.

Gabby sat on the other side of me and scooted in close, wrapping her arms around me also. It helped. A lot.

"Let me see your ankle," Gabby said.

I lifted my pant leg and she took off my shoe and sock. My ankle had a small cut on it, but other than that, it wasn't swollen.

"It doesn't look too bad. Does it still hurt a lot?" she asked.

"Not t…too much," I stuttered.

I looked up for a second. The clouds were darker, and several more had accumulated over the past several minutes.

"Was that a raindrop?" Gabby said.

"Oh, no," Lena groaned as rain belted down on us. It was so sudden, as if someone up in the sky held a giant bucket over us and dumped it out right on top of our heads. And, if that weren't enough, lightning bolted through the sky, making the three of us jump. I may have let out a scream. Three short seconds later, thunder roared, reminding us that we were alone and scared in the middle of a lake on a little metal boat, not really even a boat, more of a dinghy, with a bad motor. God, I was going to die pregnant. I wanted Asher.

Chapter Twenty-Seven

Asher

Brodie, Jackson, and I had left early in the morning to head to Redding. Brodie said it was the closest place with any decent music stores when he'd asked me if I wanted to go. He needed some new guitar strings, and Jackson wanted to pick up some more music sheets.

I jumped at the chance to get away. Not being able to talk to Mel was driving me crazy. We stayed in Redding after the music store, deciding to grab some lunch. I was glad to have the opportunity to hang with them some more. I knew Mel was anxious to leave, though she hadn't come right out and said so, considering she wasn't talking to me. But I could tell.

This trip had been a bittersweet journey. I'd finally gotten to meet my brothers, whom I'd hated most of my life until now, but I'd lost my best friend somewhere along the way. I knew she would eventually speak to me, but I didn't think we'd ever get back the close relationship we had. I didn't know what I was going to do without her. I was sure she'd let me be in the baby's life, but I wanted more than that. I didn't care about the baby so much. Wait, that didn't come out right. I did care about the baby. Of course, I cared about it, but not like I cared about Melody. She was my life. My best friend and...I loved her. Oh, God, I loved her so fucking much. I always had. Why hadn't I seen it before? I needed to fix this, and I needed to fix it today.

Mel was going to listen to me even if I had to tie her to the bed.

Brodie, Jackson, and I had lunch at a small outside burrito cafe. Brodie said it was his favorite place to eat whenever he came up to Redding. While I ate the best damn burrito I'd ever had, I got an idea, but I was going to need the help of my brothers to pull it off.

Lucky for me, they agreed.

It was a long ride home, particularly when the rain started pelting down. We could barely see the road. I was glad we were in Brodie's monster truck though with its large wheels and jacked-up frame. Some of the puddles we'd whizzed through with ease resembled small lakes. My truck was big, but not as raised as his, and my tires were more for street usage. After all, I *did* live in the city. There wasn't much use for big-ass tires eating up my gas going up and down those hills. If we had been in a regular car, or even an SUV, we'd have gotten stuck.

We pulled onto the gravel drive heading up to the farmhouse. I was excited to see Mel, but somewhat anxious.

"The house is dark," Brodie said. "There should be a light on somewhere."

"Maybe the power is out," Jackson suggested.

We all got out of the truck and made a beeline for the front porch. Even though we all ran, we still managed to get soaked. The rain came down so hard; it stung when it hit my skin.

Brodie turned the knob on the front door. It didn't open, so he got his key out and unlocked it.

"Gabrielle?" He called out, but she didn't answer. He hit the switch on the wall and the lights came on.

"Maybe she's at my house," Jackson said.

"Maybe, but she usually leaves a note," Brodie said, checking around the living room for some sign of a message from Gabby.

"I'm going to go up and check on Melody." I headed out the back door and ran up the stairs, taking two at a time. The door to the cottage was locked. I dug into my pocket, retrieved the key, and stuck it in the keyhole. I opened the door. The cottage was dark. I hit the switch on the wall and light illuminated an empty room. Mel was nowhere in sight. I ran back down the steps and caught Brodie and Jackson just as they were heading out the driveway.

Brodie stopped the truck, and I jumped in. "Melody's not up there."

"She's probably with Lena and Gabby," Jackson said.

I nodded. "Yeah, you're probably right." I hoped.

"Something doesn't feel right," Brodie admitted. "Gabrielle always leaves a note if she goes out close to dark."

It only took a minute, and we were coasting into Jackson's driveway. Brodie cut the engine and we sat there looking at another dark house. Jackson glanced around. "Lena's car is gone."

We all got out and ran through the rain to his front door. Jackson unlocked it. We went in and Jack turned on the light.

"Lena!" he yelled, but, of course, there was no answer.

I glanced around at the chocolate-brown leather sectional sofa. One of the recliners had been left in the up position as if someone had left in a hurry, but that may have just been my imagination going wild with worry since Jackson hadn't seemed too concerned about that and hadn't mentioned it. A tall floor lamp in the corner illuminated the room with a soft glow.

"Woof, woof." Rufus came barreling into the room, sliding to a halt when he reached Jackson.

"What's up, boy? Where's Lena?"

"Woof," he barked at the mention of Lena's name. Jackson scratched him behind the ears then took off up the stairs, calling out Lena's name. Rufus plopped down and stretched out at my feet.

Jackson came back down, shaking his head. "She's not here."

"I don't like it. I'm calling the bar. Maybe someone there knows where they are," Brodie said and took out his phone, hit a couple of buttons, and said, "Hey, Derrick...yeah, it's a hell of a storm. Have you seen Gabrielle or Lena...or Melody?..." He shook his head at us. "Okay. If they come in there, call Jack or me...Don't know yet...Yeah, yeah, I'll keep you posted." He hung up.

"Nothing?" Jack asked.

"Nope."

"I hate to be a pessimist here, but what if something happened to them. This storm is fucking nuts," I said.

"Let's go," Jackson said.

"Where?" I asked.

"I don't know. Come on Rufus. Let's go find Lena."

Rufus barked again and jumped to his feet.

"Man, I didn't think that dog could move that fast," I said.

Jackson grabbed Lena's scarf off the hall tree. "Rufus is a hound dog, one of the greatest trackers this side of the Turtle Lake. If they're in trouble, he'll find them."

"He's done it before. Hopefully, he'll do it again," Brodie said and slapped me on the back. "Come on, little brother, Let's go find our women."

I smiled at the little brother comment, though the sentiment didn't last long with me as my mind reeled with all sorts of possible catastrophes involving Mel and the other two women, who were my sisters-in-law.

We drove down a dark, narrow street a short distance from the house. The road soon turned to dirt. The headlights beamed, and up ahead a short distance stood what looked like a car.

"That's Lena's car," Jackson said, pointing up ahead.

Brodie pulled up beside the empty vehicle and cut the engine.

"Thank God," I muttered. "But where are they? I'm assuming they are all together."

"They have to be," Brodie said. "Gabrielle's car and your truck are still at my house."

"Right," I agreed, though my stomach knotted and I wanted to hurl. The burrito I'd had earlier wasn't mixing well with the angst of Melody missing. Possibly hurt. Seeing Lena's vacant SUV didn't help. But maybe we were close.

"Come on, Rufus." Jackson held Lena's scarf out for Rufus to sniff. "Go find Lena."

Rufus took off running, and we ran after him.

"Why the hell are they out in this storm?" I asked.

"I don't know," Brodie said.

Rufus ran to the grassy area by the lake, stopped, and howled. "He found something!" Jackson yelled. We ran toward the dog. Rufus stood on top of a blanket and a paper bag full of soaked cheese and salami. "It looks like they had a picnic." He glanced over to his left. "Oh, no."

"What?"

"The boat is gone."

"You have a boat?"

"It's just a small fishing boat with an outboard motor."

"An old fishing boat with an even older motor," Brodie supplied.

"They must be out on the lake. I forgot to tell Lena that the motor was acting up. I noticed it a few days ago when I came out to fish."

"Woof, woof, woof." Rufus took off down the beach, barking. We followed him. About a mile down, Rufus stopped and pointed his face toward the water. He barked some more, and when we reached him, we heard screams and shouts coming from the middle of the lake, but we couldn't see anything. The rain was coming down in buckets, and visibility was almost nothing.

"I see them!" Brodie shouted and waved his hands in the air. "Gabrielle!" He jumped up and down, and Rufus barked some more.

Jackson yelled for Lena. I kept shouting for Melody, jumping, waving. I was extremely excited and relieved that we'd found them. Though, we didn't know how to get to them.

Jackson tugged his phone out of his pocket and pushed the slider over, then pressed another button. "Doc. We need your boat...Meet us at the fishing hole...Of course, the same old one…I know it's raining…The girls are out in my old dinghy and the motor crapped out. They're stuck in the middle of the lake…Okay. And Doc? Hurry, it's fucking cold out here."

By the time Doc arrived with his boat and we managed to get the girls in, it was completely dark. The rain had let up some, but it didn't stop. The women were all drenched.

"Asher…" Mel slurred my name as I lifted her out of the dead boat and into Doc's. "I'm so…c…c…cold." Her teeth chattered rapidly. Lena and Gabby weren't in much better shape. "I fe…fe…fell in. I ca…ca…can't feel my toes."

I wrapped a blanket around her and pulled her tightly against me. "You're safe now."

"Saffff," she uttered, pressing her head against my chest and closing her eyes. God, her skin was red, almost as if she had a sunburn, and I was astonished at how cold her hands were when I covered them with mine. Her arms and cheeks were freezing, and I tried my hardest to rub some warmth into her.

We took them all straight to the emergency room. Lena and Gabby checked out okay, but Mel was so cold, they worried about her physical condition since she had fallen in the lake and had gotten soaked through and through. When they found out she was pregnant, they decided to keep her overnight. I stayed with her. They wrapped her feet and legs in heated socks and blankets and put some warm mittens on her hands, then covered her with more heated blankets.

She slept most of the time. I sat in the chair in the room and couldn't take my eyes off of her. I couldn't leave. This whole thing, being here in the hospital, reminded me of my mom and those last few days before she died. I couldn't lose

Mel. She was all I had. Everyone I'd ever loved had been taken away from me. I couldn't lose her, too. Yeah, I had brothers now, but that love still needed to be earned. Nurtured. Love didn't happen instantly just because you were blood. I couldn't say I didn't love them, but I couldn't say that I did either. At least not yet.

I'd had something special planned for tonight with Mel, something to fix *us*. But it would have to wait. My babies—Mel and my actual baby—needed to rest and recuperate a little while first. So, I waited and watched.

Chapter Twenty-Eight

Melody

I was rocking, gently. Lying on something, drifting with the current. No. No. Asher had found me. I was safe. I think. Dreaming maybe? A child's voice called to me. "Mommy!" That was impossible. My baby wasn't born yet. I wasn't even very far along. "Mommy!" My eyes shot open. I looked up to a ceiling I didn't recognize. I glanced around. The room was dark, and I struggled to move, but my legs were weighed down with something heavy or secured somehow. Panic took hold and I thrashed my arms to try to free myself.

"Hey," Asher whispered close to my face and grabbed my arms, gently tugging them down onto the bed. "I'm here. It's okay. You're going to be okay."

"Asher?"

He smiled at me and I swallowed. "Where am I?"

"You're in the hospital. You were so cold and lethargic; the doctors wanted you to stay overnight." I looked at the blue mittens on my hands and pulled them off. I didn't know why I had mittens on, and I wanted to see my fingers, to make sure they were all there.

My palm instantly went to my abdomen as I thought of the baby. "The baby? What about the baby?"

"Our baby is fine." He smiled. He'd said *our* baby. Had I heard him correctly? Okay, that did not slip by me.

I closed my eyes with relief.

"Asher, I…"

"Shhhh. Rest."

"Is it tomorrow?" I asked, not wanting to stay in that bed any longer, but all I got was a puzzled looked from Asher. "You said overnight. So is it morning?"

"Almost."

"You stayed here all night?"

"Yeah."

"Is that all you can say is, 'yeah?'"

He laughed. "Yeah." He placed his hand on top of mine and looked down at our hands.

"I'm just so glad you're okay. I don't know what I would have done if something happened to you. I know this isn't the best time…"

"No, don't. I've been stupid."

"Maybe." He chuckled. "But let me finish. I've been sitting here all night thinking about things. Thinking about you, about *us*. I thought I'd lost you, Mel, and I couldn't bear it. So, though this might not be the best time, I need to say this now, because I'm learning that you need to live life as if it's your last day, last hour, last minute on earth, making the most of it, living it moment by moment, because you never know when it's all going to be over or someone you love is going to be taken from you. Ever since you and I made love that first time, I've had trouble getting you out of my head. I mean, you've always been there, but it became different for me after that night. You had me completely undone. I became jealous about Alex to the point where I couldn't think straight. After you'd gone to the concert with him, I saw the way he treated you the next night and I knew he'd hurt you."

"He did, but not the way you think."

I shook my head. "I know that now. I should have known then, but love has a way of blinding you sometimes."

Did he just say *love*?

"And it makes you do and think things that you normally wouldn't. The last time you and I made love …before we found out about this"—he splayed his fingers gently over my stomach and smiled—"I wanted to keep you there in bed with me forever and never let you go. I realized then how much I needed you in my life. I didn't just say I needed you, I meant it. That night after we'd talked to Jackson and Brodie and revealed who I was, I had planned to tell you that I loved you, but then, when we found out about the baby, it just seemed like the wrong time and I didn't know how to deal with it. The thought of Alex touching you turned me into a green monster, and I had horrible thoughts, to the point of forgetting that *I* was the one you slept with first. I hadn't even taken into consideration the fact that you had the good sense not to be with Alex. I should have realized that when I knew you were home early from your date with him, but the news of Ted made things all messed up, and I didn't even think about it. Then, when I saw him in the club, I knew he was crass, knew he didn't give a fuck about the women he'd been with. But the more I remembered about watching him that night, the more I realized that I never saw him look at you, which if he had slept with you, he would have. So, I should have realized then that you turned him down. So, I'm sorry for acting like a jealous imbecile. I love you, Mel. Can you forgive me?"

I wiped the tears from my cheeks. The three little words coming from Asher's lips were so unexpected. I knew he cared for me, we were very close, but love? He actually loved me? Only in my wildest dreams would I have ever imagined hearing those words come from his mouth. Words I'd dreamed of hearing so many times. I bit my bottom lip.

"Mel? Do you forgive me?"

I nodded. "I'm sorry, too."

"Baby, you don't have anything to be sorry for."

"Yes, I do. I'm sorry I treated you like shit all week and never let you explain your feelings to me. I was so hung up on my own that I forgot about yours and that's inexcusable."

"It's very excusable after how I reacted."

I sighed and propped myself up on my elbows. "I want to get up. I'm feeling better and I want to get out of here." I sat up in the bed and swung my legs over the edge.

"Wait. I'm not finished."

"What?"

"I'm not finished. I have more to say."

"Okay."

He reached into his pant's pocket and pulled out a tiny black box then knelt down on one knee in front of me.

"Asher, what are you doing?"

"I'm asking you to marry me. I love you. I know this isn't the most romantic place to ask you to marry me, but I don't want one more second to pass by before I know the answer. Melody Grace Stevens, will you be my wife?"

He opened the small box and inside was the most beautiful ring I'd ever seen. A rather sizable diamond surrounded by a frame of smaller diamonds set in a gold band.

"My God, Asher, where did you get the money for that?"

"Don't worry about the details, Mel, just answer the question."

I looked up into his soft, green eyes and nodded. "Yes. Yes, I'll marry you."

"Really?"

"Yes, really. I've always loved you, Asher."

"You have?"

"Yes, my whole life, and I would love to be your wife."

I threw my arms around him, and he stood, pulling us both up to a standing position before crushing his mouth to mine. The kiss started heavy, then went tender as he placed his palm over my stomach again. He eased back so that his face was an inch from mine. "I love this," he said, smiling. "I'd planned to tell you that I loved you the night we found out about the baby. I had every intention of asking you to marry me that night—with or without a ring—but I held off. I didn't want you to think I was asking because of the baby, though, because I think it's nothing short of a miracle, and I'm so fucking stoked that you're going to have my child, Mel. I just want you to know that I'm not asking you to marry me because of it. You have to believe that. I loved you way before that."

"Me, too. I love you, too."

Chapter Twenty-Nine

Asher

"All packed?" I asked Mel.

"Yep." She stood in front of her suitcase with a bright smile on her face. God, she was beautiful.

By the grace of God, her morning sickness had seemed to subside. Good thing, because we were leaving in the morning. It had been four days since Mel had gotten out of the hospital, and like her, I was ready to head home. We dreaded telling her mom about the unplanned pregnancy—despite how happy we were—but knew we needed to. We decided to wait until after we told her about that and the engagement to plan a small wedding.

"I think it would be a good idea to have a plan set before we tell your mom," I suggested.

"You're probably right. We have the entire car ride home to figure it all out. I don't need a big fancy wedding or anything."

"What?" I scoffed. "Of course, we do. I mean, I do. I want it all, Mel, all the bells and whistles. The music, the dancing, the flowers, the flower girl, the ring bearer, the cake, the people. Not everyone, but some."

She laughed. "I don't know any little girls that could be a flower girl or boys for a ring bearer."

"Well, maybe we could rent them or something."

Mel didn't think that she needed a big fancy wedding with all the bells and whistles, but I put my foot down on that. We didn't need a big wedding, but it could still have all the fancy-schmancy bells and whistles. No way was I going to marry her and have her regret anything. I supposed that went both ways. I was a guy, and guys didn't usually care about elaborate weddings, but I must have been slapped by the frilly fairy because I wanted it all.

Brodie and Jackson decided to throw a party at the bar for our last night in Turtle Lake. Calling it an engagement party for Mel and me. She looked radiant, standing there in a pink dress. It had long sleeves and a rather low-cut bodice, which showed off her slightly larger than normal breasts. I guessed that was a baby thing. I liked it. They weren't actually bigger, but they were plumper. I'd been reassured by my brothers that they would get even larger as the months went by.

"How the fuck do you know?" I asked Brodie.

"I read about it."

"It's true," Jackson chimed in. "Lena has mentioned a few times that she can't wait to get pregnant so her boobs get bigger." He shrugged. "Though, I'm fine with the way the are."

Mel and I didn't know most of the people at the gathering, but everyone was full of congratulations and well wishes for us. Everyone oohed and ahhed over Mel's ring. I'd picked it up in Redding the day I went with Brodie and Jackson. The day I'd almost lost the love of my life. They'd offered their vote of approval at the jewelry store.

After a couple of rounds of shots, all except Mel, we went up on the small stage with the rest of the band and performed a couple of numbers. It would be my last time playing my brothers, and it was a bittersweet feeling of joy and sorrow. It was amazing to me how much alike Jackson, Brodie and I were. Even with different mothers, it was clear that our father's genes definitely dominated over our mothers'. We all had his green eyes, his dark, curly hair, even though Jackson's was a bit straighter and his nose was straighter, too. We all loved spicy foods—the spicier, the better—and we all wore the same size shoes.

Though Brodie and Jackson told me that it wasn't necessary to do the paternity test, I did it anyway. I figured they'd brought it up; I might as well do it. I didn't have the results back yet. They said it would take about four weeks. I wasn't worried about it. I knew.

Mel and I were sitting at a table with Brodie and Gabby, talking about nothing important. Brodie had told me about a faster way home through some back roads if I wanted to take them. Mel sipped on some sparkling cider and chit-chatted with Gabby. Jackson and Lena were sitting at the end of the bar, seeming very intense, as if they were talking about something very serious. Jackson smiled and kissed her then picked her up and swung her around before placing her back down.

He clinked his glass to get everyone's attention. "Yo, everyone. I have some news. I'm going to be a dad!"

"What about me?" Lena giggled.

"Oh, yeah, my wife, she's going to be keeping the little guy warm for eight more months."

"Congratulations!" many shouted.

"So, it's a boy?" I heard one lady ask. I couldn't remember her name, but she'd been helpful when we were rescuing the women from the lake. She stood by Doc and grabbed his hand. I guessed they were a couple.

"Hell if I know. Do we know that, Lena?"

She giggled. "No. We don't know yet."

Jackson and Lena walked over to us. "Congratulations," I said.

"Looks like my little brother won't be the first to pass on the family name after all."

"You were worried about that, were you?" I asked, sort of joking.

"Not really, well, maybe a little."

"Typical," Brodie said. "Jackson's always had to be the first to do everything."

"Not by much," Lena offered and winked at Mel. "My due date is June 10th. Mel's is June 30th. If your baby comes early or mine comes late, we could possibly go into labor at the same time. That's why I had the pregnancy tests available. I was taking one almost daily, but they kept coming out negative until yesterday. I went to the doctor this morning and they confirmed it."

Lena and Mel embraced then Gabby wrapped her arms around both of them. "It's your turn now, Gabby." Lena laughed.

"Whoa, wait a minute." Brodie put his hands up with his palms facing out, shaking his head no. "Are you?" He looked at Gabby.

"Don't worry, Brodie. You're safe."

"I'm not worried, babe." He draped his arm around Gabby's shoulders. That would just be too weird if all three of you were pregnant at the same time."

We left the party early, well, earlier than most. I feigned a headache. I needed some serious alone time with Mel before we headed back to San Francisco tomorrow.

When we entered the cottage, I saw that the bed was down. Mel must have put it down earlier and left it. We'd been pretty good about putting it up in the wall. The place was so small, and when it was down, there wasn't much room to maneuver.

She seemed different. Relaxed. Beautiful. Very beautiful. Maybe it was being pregnant. They say pregnant women are radiant, maybe it was just the way she looked at me now, or maybe it was just the way I looked at her.

"C'mere," I said and grabbed Mel around the waist, pulling her in tight so that her breasts pressed against my chest. I'd been extremely cautious about touching her or prompting any type of sexual activity the past couple of days. I wanted to make sure she was fully recovered from the boat ordeal. But enough was enough. She was fine. I was fine. I tilted her head up to mine and brushed my thumb over her bottom lip.

"Remember the shower?" she whispered.

I gave her a crooked half-grin. "I'll never forget it."

"Well, I'm feeling sort of dirty right now."

"You are?" I feigned shock, but couldn't contain the grin.

"Yeah. Real dirty."

"Right now?"

"Mmmm hmmm. I am. I think I should take some time and get cleaned up."

"That's probably a smart idea."

"It's going to take a lot of work. I want to make sure to get every single nook and cranny."

"I could help."

"I'm counting on that."

I pressed my lips over hers.

"You're going to need to take these off," she said, tucking her fingers inside the waistband of my pants and grinning against my mouth.

I liked this new Melody.

Chapter Thirty

Melody

I undid Asher's belt and let it hang there undone. I stepped back to take a look at him. He was like an exquisite portrait that needed to have its final touches painted on. I stepped back to him and stuck my fingertips under the hem of his t-shirt to lift it. Slowly. Carefully revealing each ripple of his six-pack one at a time, inching up to unveil the taut muscles of his pecs. His eyes were on mine, and mine on his. As if he couldn't wait any longer, he tugged the shirt from my hands and lifted it up over his head, tossing it somewhere on the floor.

I let my fingertips skim down his chest, being sure to go over his hardened nipples, touching him oh so slightly until I got to the top of his pants. He stood, watching me. This was the opposite of the first time we were together, when I'd stood, watching him undress me. The night he'd helped me lose my virginity.

I unbuttoned his pants and pulled the zipper down. He bit his bottom lip, and I licked mine in anticipation. I shoved his pants down, and he stepped out of them. His erection bulged in his boxer shorts, and I pulled them down, freeing his hard, perfect cock into my hand. I stroked it a few times then got down on my knees and kissed the tip before sliding my tongue out, licking around his thick head and into the slit. I felt his hand on my head, but he didn't push me, just massaged as I took the tip into my mouth, I continued to swirl my tongue around then I opened wider and took more of him in. He moaned, and I made some mmmm sound of my own as I sucked. He seemed to like that as he gently placed his hand on my head urging me down a little. Not too hard, though, just enough to let me know he wanted more. I was new at this, and he knew that. I took him in as far as I could before pulling back out, then took him in again. I sucked and watched him as I did. His eyes were on me, and I wondered what I looked like. My hand went tightly around him, pumping as I sucked.

"Mel," he huffed. "I'm going to come if you don't stop."

I didn't respond. I just kept sucking, sliding my mouth and tongue up and down on him. I wanted him to come. I wanted him to come in my mouth, I wanted to taste him the way he'd tasted me. He reached down and tugged my top up to my neck, exposing my breasts. He took one of the nipples between his finger and thumb, twirling and pinching and massaging.

"Mel, I want you," he growled in a deep voice.

He pulled himself out from my mouth and picked me up so that I was standing. My hand went to his cock, taking the place of my mouth. He kissed me. Our tongues darting around each other in a frenzied dance. Then he pulled my top over my head. He quickly unbuttoned my pants and shoved them down my thighs to my ankles, and I stepped out of them. My underwear went with my pants wherever Ash had tossed them. He shoved me back onto the bed. It was a gentle shove, but I pulled him against me as we fell onto the mattress. I grabbed his cock again, determined to finish what I'd started. "I want to taste you, Ash," I said before taking him back into my mouth. I looked up at him as I licked and sucked the tip. Then he went in a little harder, hitting the back of my throat. I tried not to gag and kept on sucking him. My lips tightened around his thick shaft. I felt him twist his body around so that his head was opposite mine. When his tongue licked up the center of my slit, I moaned onto his cock and he gently bucked his hips. As his cock slid in and out of my mouth, he twirled his tongue around my clit. His fingers were inside of me, moving, flicking around. I was out of my mind with pleasure, and I felt myself contract and climax at the same time the warmth of his come gushed down my throat.

The room fell silent except for our breathing.

I fell onto my back, gasping, closing my eyes as I basked in the moment, reveling in the high I'd just experienced.

"Holy fuck, Mel. That was the best blowjob I've ever had."

I grinned. "That was the first time I've ever done that."

He repositioned himself so that we were face to face and he took my face in his hands and kissed me. Tender, at first, then as our tongues did their dance again, heat generated between my thighs. Asher lay flat on his back and pulled me up on top of him, my legs straddled his.

"Fuck me, Mel."

God, I loved when he said that word.

I got up on my knees and rubbed his wet cock over my clit before easing down. As if my hips had a mind of their own, they gyrated around him, sliding up and down on him as he grew thicker and longer with each movement. When the tip of his erection hit that special spot inside, I bit my lip. His hand pressed firmly around each cheek of my rear and he helped move me on top of him. "Fuck me, Mel," he said again, and hearing him made me move faster, concentrating on that one spot that his cock was hitting. That one spot that must be the G-spot I'd heard about. I screamed out his name.

"Asher, oh my God, Asher!"

My hands were behind me, my palms resting on his thighs for support as I moved. I watched his face. His eyes intense on me. He tugged me tightly forward, thrusting his hips up. I dug my fingernails into his thighs. He growled as his release filled me, mingling with my own.

We never made it into the shower. I curled into him and he tucked his leg over mine as I wedged my knee between his thighs.

"I like that."

"What?

"Having your thigh rest against my balls."

"That could be dangerous for you."

"Not if you don't make any sudden moves."

I giggled. "Promise, but just to be sure."

I turned over. He tucked me into him tightly as his arms draped me with his love.

We woke up in the exact same position.

Chapter Thirty-One

Asher

Goodbyes were never fun. Especially when you've waited your entire life to meet someone, hating them for years because you thought they had something you deserved; only to discover how much you have in common, and that they'd never really had things much easier. I'd come to learn that my father hadn't been as big a part of their lives as I'd thought. I supposed that shouldn't have been a big surprise. If I thought about it, he'd cheated on their mother, not mine. They had every right to hate me, but they didn't. They not only accepted me but also embraced me into their lives.

"We'll see you at the wedding," Jackson said as he draped his arms around me in a big hug.

"You'll get your invitation as soon as Mel and I figure it all out."

I turned to say goodbye to Brodie. He stood there and stuck his hand out. So I reached for it. He grabbed me by the shoulders and pulled me into a strong embrace. "I'm excellent at throwing bachelor parties by the way, little brother."

"Sounds great to me." I didn't mind being called little brother. In fact, it felt good, and I had a feeling that Brodie sort of liked the idea of not being the youngest anymore.

"I've already got some ideas floating around in here," he said, pointing to his head as Gabby came up beside him.

"If Brodie's going to host the bachelor party, don't count on escaping the night sober. I've witnessed the effects of his celebratory antics," Lena said, wrapping her arms around me.

Gabby came in and squeezed me tight. "Take care, little brother."

Three months later, Mel and I sat at her mom's small, wooden-topped kitchen table. Mel was sipping some hot, spiced, chai tea and I was drinking water. Actually not really drinking the water, more like just holding the glass. It gave me something to do with my hands while Mel and I sat staring at each other, waiting for her mom to say something after the news we'd just dropped on her. It had taken us three months to get up the nerve to tell her. We knew she'd be disappointed with us, and it was still so close to Teddy's death. We'd held off as long as we could, but Mel was starting to get a little tummy bulge, and if we were going to try to have that wedding with all the frills we'd been secretly planning, we needed to clue her in on everything.

Karen stood at the sink, looking out the window. She'd been standing there for about three or four minutes without saying a word. It was quite unnerving.

"You say you're approximately four months?" she asked in a quiet, reserved voice.

"Yes," Mel said.

"And you say you've been planning a wedding."

"Yes," Mel answered again.

Karen turned around and walked to the table. Then sat in the chair between the two of us. "Asher, look at me." I did, right straight into her eyes. "Do you love Melody?"

I didn't even hesitate and answered with all honesty. "With all my heart. I always have." Then I looked at Mel, who gave me the sweetest smile.

"That's good because my daughter has been in love with you since she was able to talk."

"Mom, how…?"

"A mother knows these things. You'll see. Have you been to the doctor?"

Mel nodded. "Yes, of course. I've been three times so far. I'm supposed to go again next week for an ultrasound."

Karen sucked in her lips and ran her fingers through the top strands of her hair, pulling them up and back and then letting them fall. "I don't like that you left me out of this for so long. I have experience…I could have been there for your questions."

"I'm sorry, Mom. I…we weren't sure how to tell you, and it just seemed too soon after Ted."

"Too soon? How could the news of a new life come too soon after losing another?"

Mel glanced at me then back at her mom. I guess we had that figured wrong.

"I was…ashamed," Mel said, lowering her eyes down to stare at her tea.

My eyes shot to Mel's. "Mel? I…you never told me that." God, I felt like a heel. "I'm sorry. You should have said something."

"I wasn't ashamed about it with you, Asher. I was ashamed to disappoint my mom," she clarified.

Karen placed her hand over Melody's. "Honey, I love you. Yes, what you and Asher did was irresponsible, but I'm not going to judge you. You're twenty-one, almost twenty-two. I was twenty when I had Teddy. You made love with your knight. I can't fault you for that. I can fault you for not being more careful about when you took your pills, but not for wanting to be with the man you love. You've been in love with him your whole life. I'm surprised this didn't happen sooner. How have you been feeling? Any morning sickness?"

Mel picked up her tea and sipped. "Some. In the beginning. But it didn't last too long. Oh, and Mom? Don't worry, I still have a ton of questions for you."

Karen smiled. "Okay, now, tell me what wedding plans you've made so far. I have money put away for this. And your father, he always said he would help when the time came. Have you told him yet?"

"No. I'll call him tomorrow."

I felt completely out of my element, standing in the exam room next to Mel as she lay on the narrow exam bed. The doctor spread some gel on Mel's stomach then glanced at us. "You ready?"

We nodded.

She slid the wand over Mel's tummy, and the room filled with the sound of a quick beating heart. My own heart melted as the image came on the screen. Though I couldn't really tell what it was, I knew it was a baby, but the sound of the heart beating choked me up with instant love. At that moment, I knew I had been wrong.

I was wrong to think that love took time and needed nurturing to be real, because, in that instant, there was no amount of time that I needed to know that I loved the soul that belonged to that heartbeat.

I also knew that I'd loved my brothers from the first moment I looked into their eyes, maybe even before then.

"Do we want to know the sex?" the doctor asked with a smile, her bright blue eyes encouraging.

Mel looked at me. I shook my head. "No." Because it didn't matter.

Chapter Thirty-Two

Melody

I was a nervous wreck. In a little under fifteen minutes, I would be Mrs. Asher Beaumont. My father and mother were supposed to walk me down the aisle together, but he hadn't shown up yet. Typical. He'd missed my high school graduation by ten minutes, too. My mom and I stood in a small cluster of trees by the California Academy of Sciences, hidden from the rest of the guests and Asher. Lena and Gabby were close by, keeping a lookout for my dad. Of course, they didn't know what he looked like, but I'd told them to look for a silver-haired man with a goatee, wearing a tux matching the rest of the guys. He'd be hard to miss. Lena and Gabby were both Matrons of honor. Since they were both equal in my mind. Erica had been thrilled when I asked her to be a bridesmaid. She even threw us a combo shower for the baby and the wedding. Their gowns were forest green and strapless, and they'd all worn their long hair down in cascades of curls that flowed down their backs. My own gown was a pale off-white, also strapless, with an empire waist. Perfect for hiding the bump of a tummy I now sported. I also wore my hair down, but it was laced with tiny pearls throughout my blonde tendrils.

"Mom, why don't you just walk me down by yourself?" I didn't want to wait any longer.

"Let's give him another few minutes. Everyone will wait," she said, adjusting the bodice of her own beautiful, pale green gown. I'd wanted everyone to wear green so they matched Asher's eyes, my favorite color.

My dad hadn't exactly been excited about the whole pregnancy and wedding so I wouldn't have been surprised if he was a complete no-show.

"I'm here." My dad strolled into the passel of trees and kissed me on the cheek. Taking my hands in his, he eyed me from head to toe. "You look beautiful, honey."

"You almost missed it," I said.

"Sorry. Traffic on 405," he said, looking at my mom then turning back to me. "How are you? Okay?" he asked, his blue eyes traveling to my stomach.

"Yeah, I'm fine. Nervous."

"Don't be. It'll be like a walk in the park."

"It *is* a walk in the park, Dad. We're getting married outside, over there at the Shakespeare Garden."

"Right. I knew that." He winked. "Asher is going to swallow his tongue when he sees you. Hopefully, not too hard, though. That would ruin the first kiss, right?"

"Daddy!" My dad was so freakin' corny sometimes. But I loved him, even if he had missed a few key moments in my life. But he was here now, and that's what mattered. If there was one thing I'd learned over the past several months, it was that life was precious and it was best to embrace the love that was given to us because we never knew when it might be taken away.

"Ready?" he asked.

I nodded and took his arm then placed my other arm inside my mom's and we all headed toward the garden. Lena and Gabby headed down first, then my mom, my dad and I followed. When I got close enough to see the glimmer in Asher's eyes and the smile on his face, all the butterflies and nerves settled down, completely disappearing. As we walked down the center of the rows of chairs lined with white ribbon, I glanced up. Not a cloud in the sky. Birds sang their happy songs, and trees leaves swayed with the gentle breeze coming in from the ocean.

I was glad I'd listened to Asher this time. He was right to want all the frills.

Chapter Thirty-Three

Asher

I thought I'd died and gone to heaven when Mel approached in that gown. I couldn't believe I'd wasted so many years ignoring my feelings for her. Ted had been so right, and I'd been so blind. I closed my eyes for just a second, feeling his spirit beside me along with my other two brothers. Mel and I stood facing each other, her hands in mine.

"Melody Grace Stevens, do you take Asher Becket Beaumont to be your lawfully wedded husband?" He'd already asked me a similar question, and I'd given a quick and definite "Yes, I do."

Now it was her turn, and I stood patiently, waiting for Mel's answer. She looked up into my eyes after she placed the ring on my finger. "I do."

I grinned.

"I now pronounce you husband and wife. You may now kiss the bride."

I took my wife in my arms and crushed my mouth to hers. It felt like the first time I'd ever kissed her. She tasted sweet, and I wanted to stay absorbed in the kiss with our tongues engaged in this erotic tango forever.

When I heard a whistle from beside me, I slowly eased back, and the small crowd erupted in applause. I took Mel's hand and we waltzed down the aisle, past the rows of chairs and our friends and family.

Mel and I headed for the limo that would take us to the reception. We'd talked the club where we performed into letting us have it there. Even though Mel's dad had offered to pay for most of the wedding, we didn't want to go overboard. He'd also offered us a down payment on a house if we didn't go too crazy on the wedding. We'd had no problem obliging him.

The apartment was dark when I came home. Mel had moved across the hall into my apartment right after we tied the knot. We hadn't taken her dad up on the down payment for a house yet since we weren't sure exactly where we wanted to settle. Mel had stopped performing with me about two weeks ago. The baby was due any day, and the doctor had told her to take it easy and stay off her feet.

My brother, Jackson, and his wife Lena had had a baby boy two weeks ago. They sent pictures and told us to come up as soon as we could. They named him Brodie Asher Beaumont. I was so moved by his display of unconditional love and his ready acceptance of me as his brother that I'd cried when he told me. I never thought having a nephew named after me would bring such joy. Hell, I'd never thought much about nephews period.

I enjoyed my time in bed with Mel, rubbing her stomach with lotions and oils to keep it subtle and soft then snuggling close afterwards. It had become a nightly ritual so I was surprised when I came home and found all this lights off. An alarm instantly went off in my head.

"Mel?" I called out and ran into the bedroom.

I flicked on the light and she slowly sat up. "What?" Her voice was throaty and groggy.

"All the lights were out. I got worried."

"Oh, sorry, babe. I couldn't sleep. The light from the other room kept me awake so I turned it off."

I went to her side. "You okay?"

"Yeah, yeah. Just tired."

"Okay, go back to sleep. I'm going to hop in the shower."

"Okay," she yawned and pulled the pillow over her head.

I always showered after a night at the club. I usually got hot and sweaty up on stage when I performed, and my t-shirts were like a magnet for the aroma of booze and other odors permeating the air at the club—from perfumes to the essence of weed. Not a scent I wanted Mel and the baby to have to sleep next to. The hot water felt amazing after the night I'd had. I was looking forward to snuggling in close to Mel and sawing some z's myself.

I stepped out of the shower and turned off the water, grabbing a towel from the rack when Mel came in holding her hand below her belly as though she were holding the baby up from slipping down.

"You okay?"

She shook her head as liquid dripped down her legs and pooled at her feet.

"Oh." I pushed the toilet seat cover down and helped her to sit. "I'll throw some clothes on. Just stay there." I said, pointing my finger at her to stay put and hurrying out of the bathroom. I scrambled in my closet for a shirt and shrugged into it, tugging my jeans up next without any boxers. I stepped into my black Converse, foregoing the extra time it took for socks. I grabbed her jacket off the coat tree by the door and came back, putting it around her. "Let's go."

I helped her to stand. She hadn't said a word, but I could tell she was in pain. "How far apart are they?" I asked.

"About three minutes for the past hour I think," she said. "And about a minute each time."

"Really? That's close." We were twenty minutes from the hospital and this time of night there wouldn't be much traffic, so that was in our favor. But still, I worried. Three minutes. "Why didn't you say something when I first came home?"

"I knew you'd want to take a shower," she smiled. How the hell could she be smiling? But I loved that she was. I was nervous and maybe a little scared, but I did my best not to show it.

Suddenly, another contraction came on and I glanced at the little frog clock that Mel had grabbed from my mom's house. I was glad she'd taken it. I said a silent prayer, hoping my mom was listening and maybe she could put in a good word to the big guy. This contraction seemed even stronger than the last by the way Mel was panting, and I counted.

"That was sooner than three minutes," I said.

I grabbed the small suitcase we had packed and waiting in the hallway. I had my hand under her arm, leading her to the door when she stopped. She started the rapid breathing. I breathed with her, counted in my head with her. And then, took a deep breath with her long, cleansing breath. She acted like a pro. We'd gone to all the classes and did all the exercises, everything you're supposed to do, but I was still a basket case inside.

"That one was a doozie," she said. "We should hurry."

"Okay." Fuck…me.

I got Mel in the car and buckled. She was in the middle of another contraction. They were coming every minute now. We were on the road, heading down the hill when she screamed. "Oh no!"

"What?" I glanced at her, but out of the corner of my eye, I saw that the light had turned and slammed on the brakes.

"It's coming."

"What?"

"It's coming."

"No. It can't come. Not yet. Hold on."

"Asher, I can't control it. Please. I need to push."

Fuck, fuck, fuck.

"Okay." I pulled over. *God, this can't be happening.* I pulled out my cell phone and dialed 911.

"911. What's your emergency?"

"My wife is having a baby. We were on our way and…"

"Asher!"

"The baby's coming. Now!"

"Sir, where are you?"

"We're at the corner of…" Shit. I didn't know this part of the city all that well. I looked up at the street sign, but it was backwards. "Fuck. Hold on." I stepped away from the car and went to the post with the street name. "Oak and Pierce. Hurry."

"The ambulance is on its way. Sir, stay on the phone with me. I'm going to patch you through to the medical center. The nurse will take over the call."

"Okay."

"Hello, are you there?"

"Yes, I'm here."

"What's your name?" Why the fuck was this guy wasting time asking my name? "Ash. My name is Ash."

"Okay, Ash. Mine is Tom. I'm a delivery nurse and I'm going to walk you through this. Put the phone on speaker mode and set it down."

"Okay."

"Where is your wife?"

"She's in the car." I went back and got in the car.

"Asher, the baby is coming right now. Help me pull my pants down."

"Put the phone on speaker and help your wife, the ambulance is on its way."

I put the phone down. I didn't say anything, just swiped my hand over my face and got on my knees so I could face Mel.

"Ash? Did you hear me? You're going to have to help your wife deliver that baby."

Fuck. "Yeah. I heard."

Okay. I could do this. Beads of moisture beaded on Mel's forehead. I unbuckled her seatbelt and helped her shove her pants down.

"Okay, her pants are down," I yelled into the phone.

"What's your wife's name?"

"Melody."

"Melody, you're doing great." I appreciated his sentiments, but fuck a duck. We were having a baby right here in the fucking car.

"I feel the baby's head," Mel said and grunted. With one hand on the door and the other on the middle console, she held herself up off the seat and pushed as the head came out. I felt completely helpless. There wasn't a thing I could do to help Mel.

"The head is out," I said.

"Good. That's good news, Ash. Melody, we need a big push from you so your baby can come out the rest of the way."

"Oh my God!"

"What is it, Ash. What do you see?"

"The cord. The cord is around the baby's neck."

"Okay. Don't panic. Don't push anymore, Mel. Wait. Ash, use your fingers and pull the cord away. Clear it from the baby's neck so it can continue out."

"Okay." I slipped my fingers in under the cord and pulled it out over the head. The baby's face was down, which I was glad about. "Okay. I freed the head."

"Okay. Melody. One more big push. You can do it," Tom said.

"Come on, baby. I love you," I told her as she squeezed down again and the baby slipped out into my hands."

The baby had a purplish tint. I cleaned out its mouth the best I could with a hooked finger and held it face down, rubbing it's tiny back until a couple of seconds later, it cried. "It's a boy," Mel cried, as I turned him over a little then helped her place him on her chest.

"Now what?" I asked.

"He's crying, that's good. That means his airway is clear. Ash, do you have a blanket or anything in the car?"

"Um...yeah," I said, remembering the small yellow blanket Mel had packed in her overnight bag. I reached into the backseat and tugged on the bag, unzipped it, and searched for the blanket. Everything inside felt the same, either soft cotton or plastic diapers and it was dark. I finally found the blanket and pulled it out.

"Ash, are you there?" the male voice came over the phone.

"Yeah. I'm here. I have the blanket."

"Okay. Just place it over the baby to keep it warm until the ambulance gets there. There's nothing else for you to do now except wait for the paramedics. Congratulations."

I felt a hand on my shoulder. "Good job." A soft female voice came from behind me. "You did great."

I beamed and looked at Mel as I placed my hand over my beautiful son.

Welcome to the world, Becket Theodore Beaumont," Mel said. I kissed my beautiful wife.

Epilogue

Asher

I came home to a room aglow with candlelight. I glanced at the number on the door to make sure it was the right apartment before I stepped inside, particularly since there was no baby crying; only the sounds of soft classical music resonated throughout the living room.

Mel glided out from the bedroom wearing a sexy, red negligee. She smiled. "Welcome home," she said, wrapping her arms around my neck and kissing me like I'd been gone for months.

I eased my head back and studied her eyes. They sparkled with radiance. "Thanks. You look amazing. Where's Becket?"

"Sleeping."

"He is?"

"Mmmm hmmm…" She pressed her lips to mine again. "I've missed you."

"I've only been gone for three hours."

"That's a very long time when someone is horny and waiting."

"You're horny?"

"It's six weeks today, Ash, and I'm ready."

"Oh," I said and smiled. I didn't need further explanation. I just picked her up and carried her over to the sofa. Becket slept in our room and I didn't want to go in there and wake him up.

I set Mel down on the sofa, but she stood back up and began to unbutton my shirt. When she got to the last button, I shrugged out of it, tossing it on the floor. She unbuckled my jeans and I let her push them down. My boxers joined my pants, and I stepped out of them. My cock pointed at her as if to say, "What the fuck are you waiting for? Get me inside."

It had been a while, and I must admit, no one was hornier than I was at that very moment. But when she tugged me down on top of her, I slowed the pace a little, lifting the gorgeous red nightgown up and over her head. She wore sexy, red, lace panties that matched the negligee. I tugged on those lacy panties, pulling them down her thighs and she slipped each foot out. Mel was still as beautiful now as she'd been nine months ago when I'd first had the pleasure of assisting her in her endeavor to lose her V card. We always referred to our first time together as me volunteering to help her lose her virginity, and I laugh almost every time I think about how selfish my proposal had been.

I wasn't about to rush this. I wanted to make sure Mel was ready and slippery. I skimmed my fingers down her stomach and between her thighs. No worries about whether or not she was ready.

"God, Mel, you're so wet already," I huffed out in a soft whisper.

She sighed a sweet, sexy, "Yes, I know," which only made me get harder and more turned on. I kissed her neck, then her breasts, being sure not to suck at those, otherwise…well, I kissed the crease just below her breasts and I made my way down to her silky folds.

I slipped two fingers inside and then slid my tongue over her clit; she bucked her hips in acceptance. She wiggled as my tongue licked and sucked at her nub until she couldn't take it anymore and she moaned so loud I thought for sure she'd wake up Becket.

"You're most definitely ready, Mrs. Beaumont." I positioned myself over her and slid my cock back and forth over her clit, driving her crazy, and she dug her nails into my tush, tugging me, urging me as I slid easily through her silky membranes. Her snug walls caressed me and contracted around my shaft, and I almost came right then. But it was too good to let it all be over so soon. I eased out so that only the tip of my cock was inside her, giving me a moment, and then pushed back in. It was futile to think I'd last very long this time. "Mel, I love you, so fucking much."

"I love you, too, Asher." Her voice was heavy and full of lust for me, and I couldn't control it any longer as I pumped hard and felt her contract tighter around me. As I did, I emptied myself into her.

"You do this every morning?" Jackson asked me as we jogged down the street, each pushing a jog stroller. I'd talked him into buying one yesterday so he could run with me while we were visiting.

"Yeah. I've been running up and down the hills in San Francisco, though. This flat stuff is nothing compared to that."

"I'm not sure it's a good idea for me to be seen with you two." Brodie ran alongside, giving us shit about looking whipped, but I didn't care.

"You're just jealous that you don't have one of these to push yet," Jackson said.

"My time's coming. Gabrielle told me last night. She's six weeks pregnant."

"That's awesome. It's nice that all our kids will be around the same age," Jackson said. "I've heard cousins are fun to grow up with. Our uncle never had any kids," he added.

"Brothers are good to grow up with, too," Brodie said, wrapping his arm around my neck in a chokehold, giving me a taste of things I'd probably missed out on as a kid.

"No doubt." I coughed, wiggling my neck free from his grasp.

"Gabrielle and I wanted to move to the beach, but last night we were talking, and I think we like the idea of raising a kid around here."

"Yeah, I agree," I said. "And that's why Mel and I decided to move up."

"That's fantastic. I'm glad," Jackson said.

"Yeah, me, too," Brodie added.

"We want to get away from the city. It was great for us when we were unattached, but we want Becket to live somewhere…not so fast-paced as the city. San Francisco is a fun place to visit or live when you're single, but I think the city can be rough on a child. I want him to be able to enjoy the peacefulness and the sounds of the country and be able to build a fort in the backyard or some other private place he can go and just be. A thinking spot. I'd always wanted a thinking spot when I was a kid. We lived just outside the city. It was okay, and Mel's mom still lives there, but we didn't have much space or safe places we could go to explore."

"Makes perfect sense. You want Becket to have a better life than you did," Brodie said.

"Yeah."

"Maybe we can help with that," Jackson offered, and I gave him a rather surprised glance. "Don't look so shocked, Ash, that's what brothers do. We help each other."

I'd spent so many years hating these two guys. So much useless time wasted, wanting something I could have easily had if I'd taken the time to find them earlier.

Now, all the hating and the jealousy I'd spent so many years perfecting was beautifully undone by my brothers and my beautiful wife and son. I had a family, and I belonged to them just as much as they belonged to me.

NOTE TO READERS

If you read this book before reading the other two books in The Beaumont Brothers series, that's okay. There are no spoilers in this book, but if you want to go back and find out how Jackson and Lena or Brodie and Gabrielle met, please check out Beautifully Wounded and Beautifully Used. They can both be read as stand-alones.

And, if you loved this book, I'm positive you will love the first two.

Beautifully Wounded, Book 1, Jackson and Lena
Beautifully Used, Book 2, Brodie and Gabrielle
Beautifully Undone, Book 3, Asher and Melody

If you enjoyed reading Beautifully Undone or the entire series of the Beaumont Brothers, please consider leaving a short review at your favorite online retailer and let others know how you liked it.

Subscribe to my newsletter via my website and receive notification about new releases and specials at www.susangriscom.com.

Follow me on:
   Facebook
   Twitter
   Instagram
   Pinterest
   Goodreads

You can also follow me on Amazon Bookbub and Bookgorilla to get notifications of new releases and deals.

THE EMOTIONAL STUFF

There are always many, many people that contribute to the publication of a book. First, I always like to thank my husband, because if it weren't for him, I wouldn't be writing. I never would have discovered that I had a passion for putting words down and forming stories without him. He gave me the opportunity to learn who I was and what I wanted. So, thank you, honey.

My kids give me inspiration in everything they do. I've always strived to be the best that I can be for them and to teach them to be the best that *they* can be. I'm proud of them and who they have become.

My mom's a strong woman and has had many struggles in her life. Her struggles are not out of the ordinary, but she has always come out the victor. She always manages to build herself up, even after all the obstacles that have threatened to take her down. I admire her so much for all she has accomplished, and thank her for being a wonderful example of what a strong woman is.

My Facebook friends. Yep. That might be you. Thanks for putting up with all my posts about my books and for reading them.

My street team members, Soul Sisters. You build me up when I'm feeling down and keep me on my toes when I need a push. Thank you ladies for all that you do to help get the word out about my books. You will always hold a special place in my heart.

My beta readers, Heidi Hudson, Kim Shaw, Kelly Hawkins, Katherine Eccleston, Crystal Allmon, Wendy Higgs, and Shannon Hunt. Thank you all so much for your early and quick reading of this book. All your suggestions were very helpful.

I owe a ton of thanks to my author buddy, Amber Garza. Every visit with you is very enlightening, and I love how you help keep me up to date with current trends.

A huge, huge thank you to my fantastic editor, Chelle Olson from Literally Addicted to Detail. You rock! You make me shine and are always there to assist with everything from helping me choose the best stupid phrase, like beat off or jacked off, which one to use or not to use, to the perfect placement of that so important comma. And let's not forget the cherry. ☺ Love you, babe.

Lastly, to you, the reader. Thank you for all of your reviews and the support you've shown throughout the years of my writing career. I love you to the moon!!! Be strong!

ABOUT SUSAN GRISCOM

Susan Griscom writes paranormal and contemporary romance. She's hooked on gritty romances and is a huge fan of superheroes and bad boys confronted with extraordinary forces of nature, powers, and abilities beyond the norm mixed with steamy romance, of course.

She loves those days when she gets to sit around in her sweat pants, doing nothing but writing emotionally charged stories about love and violence and drinking coffee.

She lives in Northern California with her romantic husband and together they have five great superhero kids and eight mini-superhero grand kids, so far.

9 781523 321353